Three Sisters

by

Susan Payne

Three Sisters

The Wild Rose Press, Inc.
PO Box 708
Adams Basin, NY 14410-0708
Visit us at www.thewildrosepress.com

Publishing History
First Rose Edition, 2020
Trade Paperback ISBN 978-1-5092-3411-0
Digital ISBN 978-1-5092-3412-7

Published in the United States of America

She would be better off without his attentions, able to do what she was really there to do without the Devil getting in the way.

"Come on, give me a name at least," he coaxed.

Hoping he would go away if she appeased him, she replied, "Call me Ginger, everybody else does. Ginger Taylor."

"Hmmm, with those eyes and that hair, I'd think an 'O' should go in front of your last name, like O'Riley, or O'Brian," he said twirling a ginger colored curl around his finger at her left temple.

Ginger smiled and replied, "Anything you say, Marshal, but I have to get back to the floor or Maurice will be yelling for me."

"Tell Maurice you have a private game upstairs. I can make it well worth your while," Devil offered watching her reaction.

He didn't need to wait long. She was up and pushing the door open into the casino before realizing she was going to move.

Calling back, she said, "I don't work above the main floor. If you want a game upstairs, Marshal, it will have to be solitaire." She left him standing in a room of laughing men.

Dedication

To my three sisters—like the Musketeers, we stuck together even when we knew one of us was wrong. Only a sister knows what I'm talking about.

Southeast Texas 1874

CHAPTER ONE

Devlin walked into the casino as usual and as usual it was unremarkable, the patrons behaving in a civilized manner, taking their losses quietly and their wins with much more enthusiasm. His gaze moved around the room, searching for anyone who may be cheating the unsuspecting townspeople, someone used to dealing from the bottom of the deck.

Feeling like he got kicked in the gut, he watched her walk out of the back room. She was tantalizingly beautiful emerging from the office where they counted the winnings for the night, the office where the owner entertained his most profitable customers with Brandy, Cognac and willing women.

The woman walked to her station by the roulette table and pasted on the come-hither smile of her trade. He went to her, like iron to a magnet. Once beside her she glanced at him, her brows rose in a question then returned her focus on the players and their bets, ignoring the man with the federal marshals' badge.

"Place your bets, gentlemen, last call to place your bets," she said in a husky voice, like a woman just waking up after a night of lovemaking.

Devlin watched her, his nether regions raising hell every time her well-modulated voice gave the last call for bets. He shifted, a little uncomfortable in his city suit, but that was what he had on when the wire came to order him to this one-cow town. A town that swelled to double its size during cattle drives.

He was glad though. He would look his best for this

woman who had unquestionably grabbed his attention and refused to give it up. Of course, she wasn't there to tempt him any more than any of the other men hypnotized by her. Placing wagers they never meant to make just so they could stay within the sound of her voice.

He was mesmerized by the enticing woman in a green gown with a scooped neck low enough to be interesting, tight enough to make sure everything interesting remained hidden. There was a fascinating crisscross of ties in the back ending at her waist, forming the material to her ribcage until it flared with the help of a sturdy corset and several petticoats. His fingers itched to unlace them. A bustle frame or maybe padding of which she had no need emphasized her womanly curves. Her figure was exquisite and womanly enough for any man. Her smooth alabaster arms were bare so she could deal without hindrance. No jewelry broke the lovely expanse of her neck and shoulders, just a dusting of intriguing freckles and small gold studs in her ears.

As the croupier raked the chips off the orange baize, the green-eyed goddess again gazed questioningly at him, but Devlin still had nothing to say, merely watched as she returned her attention to her work.

Bea's attention wasn't completely on her work as it should be due to the tall handsome man standing next to her. His dark eyes taking in her every move. It wasn't due to his attractiveness or intentness but the fact he was wearing a federal marshals' badge that she found so disconcerting. The rugged appearance of a man who spent a lot of time in the sun belied his clothing and manner. He didn't seem to notice the other women plying their trade on the customers. She also couldn't ignore the intriguing cleft in his chin and the way he could raise one eyebrow, speaking without making a sound. That eyebrow indicating a question, an answer and everything in between.

Finally, the casino owner, Maurice, wearing the de rigueur evening suit with tails, came to relieve her from the table. The handsome marshal followed her into the back area where the employees took their breaks. She had no option since she knew watching people place bets for too long made employees get sloppy. Besides, she needed to rest her feet and appreciated slipping out of the heels she wore working the floor. As usual, there were more men than women in the room.

A woman talented enough and beautiful enough to run any of the table games was rare, but then Beatrice Taylor knew she was a rare woman. She would rid herself of this man's attention and continue doing her job.

"Tell me, what's your name?" His deep timbered voice rumbled.

"What's yours?"

"Devlin, Marshal Devlin."

"Ah-h-h, the Devil. Well, I have heard of you, Marshal Devil. Aren't you out of your usual territory? I mean, I was told you only show up where there's trouble or is it that trouble shows up where you are?" She sipped the cup of coffee she poured for herself without offering him one. After all, he wasn't an invited guest. At least she hadn't invited him. She would be better off without his attentions, able to do what she was really there to do without the Devil getting in the way.

"Come on, give me a name at least," he coaxed.

Hoping he would go away if she appeased him, she

replied, "Call me, Ginger, everybody else does. Ginger Taylor."

"Hmmm, with those eyes and that hair, I'd think an 'O' should go in front of your last name, like O'Riley, or O'Brian." He twirled a ginger colored curl around his finger at her left temple.

Ginger smiled and replied, "Anything you say, Marshal, but I need to get back to the floor or Maurice will be yelling for me."

"Tell Maurice you have a private game upstairs. I can make it well worth your while," Devlin offered watching her reaction.

He didn't need to wait long. She was up and pushing the door open into the casino before he realized she was going to move.

Calling back, she said, "I don't work above the main floor. If you want a game upstairs, Marshal, it will have to be solitaire." She left him standing in a room of laughing men.

It took several minutes for Ginger to return to her normal color. Her fair skin an easy read for anyone with experience. That's why she always wore a more conservative dress when she was playing cards for a profit and not for the house.

Scanning the room, she searched for anyone needing relief. Half her evening was spent dealing at the Black Jack tables and she was waiting for one of the male dealers to raise his hand asking for a break.

Maurice motioned her over to one of the tables and Ginger noticed Devil was back on the casino floor, watching her. She hoped he would be called away or become bored with toying with her. She wasn't playing hard to get. She'd been at this type of work too long not to be really hard to get. No one had done so before now and she wasn't about to let a handsome lawman change that.

The rest of the evening progressed as usual. The Devil finally giving the casino its peace by leaving the customers to lose in private. As the casino closed table by table due to too few players, Maurice told Ginger to head home for the night.

Living in the hotel down the boardwalk, she didn't even need to cross the street. A couple of saloons were still well lit and noisy with piano music and women's laughter. She pulled her cape tighter around her bare shoulders and startled when a tall man approached, her hand tightening around the derringer she always carried in a hidden pocket in her gowns.

"I didn't mean to frighten you but I thought calling out to you would bring more attention than you wanted," Devil said meeting her and then turning to walk alongside her without touching.

"I walk home every night, Devil. You don't need to escort me and I'm not offering you anything for doing so," she replied stiffly.

"I was clumsy this evening. I'm sorry to have offended you. I made assumptions and I should know better in my line of work. Nothing and no one is what it seems," he told her, his breath showing up as little white clouds in the cold air.

"Thank you for your thoughtfulness, Marshal, but this is home for me." She turned to enter the front door of the hotel only to feel him right behind her.

She stopped, not sure what to do about this man who refused to take no as an answer. Waking-up the hotel staff to have them throw Devil out seemed improbable and impossible. Plus, she didn't want to lose her room either, not yet. It may take a few more weeks to be sure.

He stopped when she did, not wanting to run into her. Then raising an eyebrow, explained, "I'm staying here, too."

Embarrassed at her thoughts, Ginger clarified, "Sorry, just habit, I guess. I've been on my own for a long time."

"Maybe we should change that?" he offered as they climbed the stairs together.

Ginger smiled at the expected offer from the marshal. After all, he was simply a man like any other who saw a pretty woman without a male protector.

"I'm fine the way I am. I'll never depend on a man to take care of me. I find they're just a little too selfish when all is said and done." Stopping, she retrieved a key from her bag and finished, "This is my room. Thank you for seeing me home but let's not make a habit of it. I have my reputation to think of."

The tall Texan tipped his hat saying, "Certainly, ma'am, I quite understand. I'm just down the hall in room twenty-four if you need me for anything." And one sexy eyebrow raised itself in a question.

Ginger smiled at his tenacity and entered her room, making sure to lock it from the inside while he was still within hearing.

The next day at a late luncheon, Ginger was dressed in a dark blue day dress, the high neck decorated with an ivory carved brooch. The material was a heavy brocade trimmed in velvet in consideration of the cold day outside the large window having a view of the main street.

Stopping at her table, Devil asked in his deep sexy

voice, "May I join you? I find I have too many meals alone and we do know each other."

Glancing about the empty dining room she acquiesced to his request and he sat down, placing his hat on the table, brim up. The waiter hurried over and Ginger smiled at the way the other man went out of his way to make sure Devil was aware of all the services the restaurant could provide in the way of food and beverages.

"I'll take a pot of coffee and the beef steak, fried potatoes, green beans and winter squash. The same for the lady," he told the man bent over the small paper pad, nodding at every word out of Devil's mouth.

"That's too big a meal, I'll never get through all of it. I usually just have an egg and toast." Ginger said, objecting to the expensive meal and the possibility he would think her to be in his debt.

"I noticed this is your first and probably only meal of the day. You'll be going in to work in a few hours where you will be until early morning." He let his eyes roam freely over her torso. "I assume you're not slimming so the one meal is due to, shall we say, economics as to what you order. Breakfast is always the least expensive meal offered."

Ginger looked at him but said nothing to his hypothesis, because that is all it was. Complete conjecture.

At her silence, Devil continued, "You get paid well, at least three dollars a night plus tips. I saw a couple of ten-dollar chips go into that pretty little green dress last night, up against your...I'll call them your assets. So where is all the money going? Trying to get out of this small town and into a more prosperous city? I can help you if you'd like me to."

The coffee came and Ginger poured Devil a cup that he took black while she added a little sugar to hers, a habit she had gotten into when drinking cheap coffee, which was bitter, but also to get the needed energy the free sugar gave her.

"I wouldn't expect anything in return." At her disbelieving expression, he added, "Really, maybe just the chance to know you better. I'm not going to be here long. I'll have the problem cleared-up and then they'll send me elsewhere. But first, I can see you settled in a proper city. Austin? Dallas? I have a spread up near Aberdeen. Again, only if you're interested." And that eyebrow raised itself in question.

"Thank you for the offer but I make my own way. You're right, I am planning on moving on to a more exciting town," she admitted, hoping the tidbit of information would satisfy his curiosity about her.

"You seem to be quite discontent with your choices. I've gotten as far back as the City of Kansas. Then Colorado, two mining towns, wasn't it? Nevada, Louisiana, then Arizona and now Texas. Taking a tour of the territories or searching for someone?"

"Just a restless nature. I've always wanted to travel," she lied easily. He had been asking around about her, but why? What had she done to catch his interest? He was too dangerous a man to allow close to her and her secrets.

The lawman in him seemed to feel the lie, knew she was and wasn't answering his questions. "If I were to dig deeper, would I find the reason you left those fine, prosperous towns so fast? Any pilfering, blackmail or ex-husbands lurking around?"

He searched her face, meeting the fire in her eyes at

his questions. "You've got something you're hiding and if it has anything to do with this case, I'll pursue it even if I'd hate to put someone so lovely in jail. Hopefully you're merely a front, the window dressing for men doing much more nefarious things. Things you aren't aware of at this time."

"I knew I should have refused to let you sit down." Standing up, she grabbed her knit bag and stormed out of the dining room, angrier at herself than at Devil. No, she wasn't, she was mad as hell at Devil. How dare he question her life, her comings and goings? He had a lot of nerve misusing his office trying to get something to use to force her into his bed because she was sure that was what everything was all about. And she couldn't take that kind of scrutiny, not now, not when she may be this close.

A few minutes later there was a knock on her room's door and she decided to stay quiet until Devil went away, but then the voice of the waiter said, "Miss Taylor, the gentleman said you were taken ill, but that you might like your meal for later so I brought it up with some tea."

Ginger got up from the chair, opened the door and said graciously, "Thank you for your thoughtfulness. Just a moment and I have a gratuity…"

"Thank you, Miss, but the gentleman made sure to cover it. I hope you're feeling better soon." He set the tray on the table by the window and bowed slightly.

Ginger glanced at the tray with a jaundiced eye, but then thought, W*hat the hell, I was going to eat before that dreadful man interrupted me so I may as well eat now and save the rest for a meal in the morning. His loss, my gain.* She cut into the very rare, very excellent steak.

By nine o'clock the tables were filled. Not too many

places for men of money and quality to go in a town this size, and no man stays at home with his wife in the evenings. Ginger was completely engrossed in what she was supposed to be doing when she saw Devil enter.

Feeling her smile slip, she pulled strength from somewhere deep and remembered he said he wasn't here for long. She could hold all this together until he had to leave, to stalk someone else with his lustful thoughts.

Then he was at her side again, just watching, not drinking, not speaking, just watching. She searched for Maurice hoping to tell him the man was bad for business, that he was intimidating the customers merely standing there. Then she decided to take the bull by the horns.

"Look, Devil," she hissed. "Will you go away if I promise to see you after work? In the morning? I'm having trouble concentrating with you breathing down my neck."

"Yeah, I was hoping I was getting to you. I'm not unreasonable. We can work something out to our mutual benefit," he said, caressing her arm with the back of his hand.

"Don't touch me, not here." She softened, trying to figure out how she could leave before morning, before he came to claim what he thought she was offering.

Devlin withdrew his hand quickly, surprised he had the temerity to touch her in public, even if it seemed everyone was focused on their cards or numbers. She had a smile that was hard to read and Ginger's color was high with, he hoped, unleashed desire for what he was proposing.

Then a blur of gray rushed past him and into Ginger's open arms, the sobbing girl saying something about his deputy, Walker, and dead men and spending

nights together and between sobs, Devlin could see his night of passion disappear into smoke. He wanted to punch the man following the young woman, a man he recognized as his own deputy.

"What have you done to my baby sister?" shrieked Ginger as she wrapped herself protectively around the young girl, her eyes murderous, hands turned into talons to tear and defend.

CHAPTER TWO

Andy righted herself with the world although the stagecoach was still lying on its side. Pulling off her hat, she pushed her curly hair back from her face and peeked up through the side window. She searched the horizon for any sign of the men who had ambushed the Bentley stagecoach killing the driver and his guard as they tried to save the passengers and payload. The small wood bank box wedged into the foot-well was long gone.

She saw nothing of the group of robbers who had chased the careening coach until it over-turned, causing one of the horses to pitch to the side and break its leg as the rest tried continuing to run. The terror in their eyes as they tugged their dead comrade would not be easily forgotten. One of the robbers compassionately cut the harness then shot the injured horse to put it out of its misery. That's when Andy got a good look at him from the interior of the dark coach.

Unfortunately, the bandits weren't as sympathetic to the men trying to defend the coach and her. Her fellow travelers had tried to prevent more harm, ordering her to stay hidden inside. The two male travelling companions now shot dead outside the coach protecting her. She said a prayer, wishing she knew more about the men so she could write to their families and explain the circumstances of their death.

Pulling herself out through the window, she scrambled across the coach, hung over the edge then dropped to the ground. A barren desert surrounded her, only some scrub brush and a few cacti for as far as the eye could see. The road, if one could call it that, which the coach had been travelling on didn't even show. The

horses so crazed by the attack they had run uncontrolled across the desert until the lead horse went down.

Walking to the man who had introduced himself as a doctor, she hesitated then felt the outside of his suit coat, checking if there was anything to identify him or his family. As she was going through the coat pockets of the second man, a male voice nearby interrupted her.

"Even a vulture waits 'til the body's cool before picking at it," the deep voice said dryly.

Standing up straighter, Andy, with years of training in facing adversarial males replied, "That is a lie. Vultures actually will help their dinner along if it's too weak to fight. They do kill at times, not always waiting till their prey stops moving before calling the others to dine."

"You some kind of teacher or something? I was trying to point out that you're going through these dead men's pockets looking for…?" he asked getting off his horse and walking over to the two dead employees of the coach line.

A deputy's badge showed predominately on his sheepskin coat and he wore his tan ten-gallon hat pulled down shading his face. He was tall with brown hair and eyes and would be considered handsome under the two-day's growth of beard. Cowboy boots and a pair of tan trousers topped by a gun belt with a six-shooter hanging on each hip the only other things Andy took note of.

"I was searching for something that would tell me who these brave men were. They died saving me and I owe their families the truth about their deaths," she explained.

"Well, the truth is both these men are Pinkertons. I know them from previous cases. As for protecting you,

they probably were, but their first job was to protect the moneybox. Four men and none of them alive. Who the hell robbed this coach?" he asked inspecting the spot the robbers' horses trampled when one of the men got down and took the moneybox.

"They weren't Indians, I can tell you that much," Andy offered.

"Why would I think it was?" the deputy asked, studying the horses' shoeless prints and fingering the arrow sticking out of the bottom of the coach.

"It was white men pretending to be Indian braves, but one was wearing Chippewa buckskins and moccasins that were definitely Comanche. Then there was their hair. Some kind of cheap wigs on two of them while the other three tied feathers in their hair but they had barbershop cuts and shaves. Their faces were untanned where they had mustaches not that long ago. The horses weren't Indian ponies, either, and they all had full saddle and bridles, again, not an Indian raiding party. Besides, that's a Sioux arrow plunged into the coach by the man who took the box," Andy told the deputy at length what she had seen and her conclusions.

"You're sure about all this I take it? No suppositions? All based on facts?"

"I never base anything on supposition. I may begin with a hypothesis, but then all facts are left to be verified by experimentation and testing," she explained knowing her years of study would never let her assume anything as fact.

"Well, I never hypothesize, but I do think we need to get our tails out of here just in case they come back when they find out the box is empty. This trip was set up to catch these bushwhackers. It's the fifth coach of the

line targeted, so they thought it might be an inside job. Why they let you on board is a mystery to me," he said, moving the dead men closer to the coach.

"It's not a mystery. I showed up this morning to purchase a ticket. And, to be honest, the driver was hesitant to accept it, but finally allowed me to board." Andy began gathering the men's hats and other belongings to lay with them.

"I said it was kept quiet, which meant the ticket agent didn't know and to be honest, there's not many women travelling out to this area, alone. You got a husband waiting for you, Ma'am?" he asked. She saw him glance toward her left hand but knew he would be unable to detect a lack of a wedding ring beneath her kidskin gloves.

Remembering her older sister's warnings, she stayed as close to the truth as she was living it at the time. "It's Miss, Miss Miranda Taylor, but everyone calls me, Andy. I was travelling to meet up with my sister. I had, umm, slipped and twisted my ankle and couldn't travel with her. I stayed until I could get a coach heading to Lemmoxville," she explained easily, the truth and lies intertwined.

"I'm Federal Deputy Walker, but you can just call me, Walker. I'll be takin' you the rest of the way with me as soon as we get these bodies protected. The real vultures won't be far behind. They'll send a posse out as soon as the coach is an hour late, so these men will be taken back to their families," he explained piling the luggage around the bodies to keep the vermin off them. "The varmints can start on the horse's carcass first and by then the recovery party will be here."

Once the bodies were covered, the Deputy picked up

his horse's reins to mount, saying, "That's that. Let's go."

"You said you knew these men. Aren't you at least going to pray over their remains?" Andy asked, wondering about a man who could be so cold-blooded around his dead friends.

"Miss, I've been praying for these men for the last fifteen minutes of moving them over here together. Then I spent the next ten praying the SOB's that did this would die and rot in hell. I'm done praying and we need to be movin'. Besides, I never saw a woman so cool and collected after what just happened. At least I'm saved from dealing with a hysterical jittery sort," he told her holding his hand out to help her mount in front of him.

"I'm not cool but I do keep myself under control. There are things we must get through first." She walked towards him, her dress swaying femininely.

"Ah, miss, you and I can fit on this horse or your dress thing and I can fit on this horse, but not all of us can, so…." he said looking pointedly at the fashionable bustle.

"Oh, yes, of course. Give me a second." Turning, she reached up under her skirts to her waist and untied the bustle she and her sister, Trudy, had fashioned as well as the two layers of petticoats and let them drop to the ground where she daintily stepped out of them.

Walker's mouth went dry and he swallowed twice before he trusted his own voice. "I'll take those up here and we'll bury them further away. I don't want anyone knowing there was another passenger, not right away at least, until we know the inside man."

"I take it I'll need to ride astride. Easier on the horse

with the two of us, right?" she asked gathering her dress skirts and allowing Walker to hoist her onto the large horse.

Walker was left with a pile of feminine under clothes, which he stuffed partially under his bedroll. Mounted behind the thin woman who seemed to be a contradiction of everything he knew about city ladies, he pressed his knees to set his horse in motion.

The young woman was wearing a wide gray skirt covered by a darker gray cape and he knew she began the day looking fashionable and well groomed, opposite of what she appeared now. She was pretty with her wide-set hazel eyes and hair all sorts of colors like blond and red and light brown.

He watched her as they worked together earlier and she hadn't shirked from touching the dead men and making their resting place as neat and proper as could be expected out in the desert. He was intrigued by what a woman like her was doing on her own, even after the story she told him. Something seemed off with her, but he wasn't sure exactly what. He didn't think she had anything to do with the robbery or they would have taken her with them.

Walker nudged the sides of his horse, which obeyed and went perpendicular to the original stagecoach route, working his way cross-country to the town where he hoped his partner was still waiting. The horse kept an easy pace, not showing the extra effort of carrying two rather than one. Walker tried not to think about the young woman's fanny rubbing against his private parts, or the sight of her trim stocking-covered leg laying against the length of his, or the smell of strawberries if he allowed his nose too close to her hair. He ignored all those things until it about killed him.

"We'll need to stop for the night and rest the horse. I'm not as far as I'd like to be but it's as far as I dare go today." He pulled the horse to a stop and dismounted, helping Andy down.

Andy studied the ground. "Umm, I think we need to move a little way from here."

Walker, a little on edge after having ridden hours half-aroused, said, "Look, we don't have time to set up the perfect camp. We need to get something that will burn to keep us warm and maybe something to eat."

"I understand our needs but those holes and marks indicate we are standing in a middle of a nest and I do not wish to wake-up with dozens of scorpions up my skirts."

Looking around his horse's hooves, Walker realized she was right.

"Sorry," he said as he walked the horse away and Andy followed, watching to make sure none of the little bastards attached themselves to her skirts.

Rubbing his eyes, he said, "I'm more tired than I thought. I rode straight through from another assignment and am supposed to meet up with my marshal. He'll be very interested in a group of men posing as Indians robbing coaches." They walked and then checked the area for any previous tenants before setting up camp.

The horse was unsaddled and tied to a branch close enough for it to get the dried grass and maybe the dew in the morning. Andy must have stayed close to the area they surveyed but she had pretty much gathered all burnable materials by the time he came back with a skinned and dressed hare and a couple of larger dried branches.

"Can you cook?" he blurted out when he came upon her starting the campfire pile with a flint lighter.

"On a stove. I'll try over a campfire, but do we have anything to cook? Besides the rabbit, I mean? I can fashion a spit, I think, if you can help me push these two sticks into the dirt. It's pretty dry and hard," she said picking out two sticks with a second branch off them, which she used to hold the thicker stick she pushed through the rabbit's cavern.

Wilder watched with some amazement. This woman came across like a china doll, porcelain skin, a little cherry-pink bow mouth, a small nose and large hazel eyes fringed with dark lashes yet she didn't whimper or act squeamish. She did what needed to be done without whining or placing blame. He kept waiting for the dramatics or hysterics or any other 'ics'. How often does a woman fall into the happenings of today? So how come she isn't a whimpering puddle he had to cajole into good spirits?

The fire was started and the little rabbit looked forlorn above the small pile of branches and leaves. There were plenty of dead grasses, but they burned smoky, not fiery and there wasn't going to be much to keep them warm tonight.

They finally got the fire hot enough to cook the rabbit. Andy took one of the hind legs and gave the rest to Walker.

"You gave me more than half," he began to argue.

"You're doing more than half the work. My body needs less to live on and I have some fat reserves you don't. You're all muscle. I'll be fine for several days yet and I figure we'll run into food before then," she spoke without guile.

"It don't seem right. You're the woman."

"And I am in need of you. Without you, I will wander around in this desert area until I die of thirst or hunger," she explained reasonably. She chewed the small bits of meat from the bone and then sucked on the end, placing the knuckle of the leg in and out of her mouth.

Walker was almost done with the rest of the hare when he realized he hadn't taken his eyes off Andy as she worried the bone with her small, pearly teeth. He gave her a drink from his canteen before taking one himself. The metallic flavor of the water turned sweeter with the taste of her lips on the opening when it came to his turn to drink.

The two went their separate ways to conduct the necessary functions and then the rest of the night had to be faced. Walker laid his bedroll, a thin canvass tarp and blanket that would help keep the earth's cold from seeping into their bones, on the ground near the now glowing ashes of their fire.

"I'll lay down facing away from the fire and you curve against me and we'll cover us both with the cape. That way what's left of the fire will keep your back warm and I'll keep the front warm." Then he lay down curved away from her, his guns and rifle lying in front of him.

Exhaustion overtook them both but the morning found them in completely opposite positions. Andy was curved towards the lifeless fire and Walker was covering her protectively, the gray cape still in position over them both.

Walker was the first to waken, his arousal plainly nestled up against her fanny, happy and content, well almost content with its warm home. He forced his body away, but Andy snuggled back up against his warmth, evidently finding the cold morning air unwelcome.

Forcing himself to pull away from the inviting body, he said, "Time to get going. We may make it to a little town I know by this evening."

After dispersing the cold ashes and taking care of morning functions, the two mounted the horse and began another long day together. Walker both hating and loving the rocking motion of the horse as it moved along, making Andy's fanny rock along with it.

They stopped to rest the horse a couple of times and both had taken sparingly of the canteen, giving the horse some water, also. Finally, as the sun was setting, a few buildings appeared on the horizon and the horse sped up, recognizing the chance for the companionship of other horses and grain.

Walker went directly to the livery pushing Andy into the shadows, not wanting anyone to see her. "I'll take the horse inside to get some feed and water. Can you stay out here until I make sure no one dangerous is inside? This has always been a stop-off for men on the run and they don't follow the normal rules of society."

"I'll stay here until you get back," Andy said without argument.

Dropping off his horse with a coin, he went over to the saloon, about the only activity going on in the town. The sheriff's office door was closed and covered with cobwebs indicating the town was without a lawman again. The few brave men who had accepted the job often didn't live long enough to collect their pay at the end of a month and the ones who did put in their resignation at the same time. Walker understood these border towns. Just tame enough to offer a few amenities and wild enough to allow like-minded criminals to live in freedom.

As he entered the smoky room, a slatternly sort of woman who always seemed to run such establishments met him in front of the bar. Trying to discern the kind of cash he had to spend and what his appetites were, she smiled broadly.

"Hi, honey, you're a long drink of water now, ain't cha?" she said, rubbing his shoulder and leaning into his hip with her pelvis.

Scrutinizing the room, he found the usual roughly made bar, several tables and a number of mismatched chairs. Many of them occupied with men who looked suspiciously like the posters tacked up on the jail's wall back home.

He took note of the barman, a burly middle-aged man missing a couple of front teeth, and the woman bent over the table in the corner while some man groped her from behind. Most of the other men at the table ignored her preoccupation.

Walker was glad he had made Andy wait by the livery. This place was either worse than he remembered or his ability to over-look certain aspects of life has been compromised by having Andy with him.

Reaching into his pocket, he took out a couple of coins and began to sort out the right one when the woman, still rubbing up against him said, "You must be pretty randy or green fella. You pay after your fun here. You're kinda' old to be getting your cherry popped so I figure it's just been awhile?"

Annoyed at himself for letting his guard down with the woman, he said angrily, "Not for that. I need to buy a couple of blankets." After glancing around again added, "The cleanest you got."

The older woman let go of Walker's arm realizing she wasn't going to get any money off him for services rendered and yelled upstairs, "Blanch, throw down a couple of blankets out of the closet will ya?" Then to Walker said, "These just got back from the laundry so they're as clean as a licked nipple."

Walker grunted in acknowledgment and asked, "You got any food around here besides these pickled eggs?" The bartender shook his head.

"I'll take a couple of soda waters and that half bottle of whiskey." He threw a coin to the barman and took the eggs in the wooden bowl.

Walker walked back unable to see Andy behind the livery and was about to call out when he saw a movement near the building next door. Turning, he saw her face, a white oval in the moonlight and went to her. She was shivering, but not complaining which he had become used to accepting as her way.

"I had to move," she explained. "The livery man came out to relieve himself."

He opened one of the blankets that were surprisingly thick and wrapped it around her slim frame like a second cape. Offering her the bowl of four eggs, she took one and began to eat it, taking small bites and holding the food in her mouth longer than necessary. Walker did the same, knowing this would be it for the next twenty-four hours. He bit into the last of the eggs before giving the last bite to Andy. She hesitated, but then accepted the morsel from his fingers.

"I think we should leave the horse in the livery and find someplace for us to sleep. Neither the so-called hotel nor the saloon will be safe for you. You're too much a

Susan Payne

lady plus you're too young to be ignored by this crowd."
He thought a moment more and then said, "I know the
place. Not much warmer, I'm afraid, but better than
outside on the ground."

Leading Andy through the shadows, they crossed
the road, knowing everyone awake seemed to be at the
saloon. The piano and loud talk audible down the street.
Walker went to the door of the jail and tried the latch. As
most jails, the key to this door was long gone. No one
bothered to lock a jail only the cells and, in this town,
that hadn't been done in a while.

Andy followed him into the cell without questioning
his plan, letting him take down the cobwebs and scare
away any mice or other things that may have made their
winter home in the otherwise clean room. She may work
on facts upheld by experiments and testing, Walker
worked on instinct.

As she peered around in the gloom of the cell she
admitted, "I don't comprehend your concept of working
on your gut, but I know your instincts are honed from
years of experience, hence testing, and I will follow it
unless my own knowledge tells me you're wrong."

"Here, this will warm you up," he said offering her
the unstopped bottle of whiskey. Andy hesitated then
took a swig, losing her breath in the process.

Gasping, she said, "I feel a wave of warmth going
all the way through my body, all the way to my toes."

Walker took a longer pull on the bottle before
placing the cork back in it.

Picking up the only mattress, he shook it then placed
it back on the ropes tied between the two stringers on the
cot. Andy didn't hesitate when he motioned for her to lay
down first as he went to lie on the floor beside her.

24

"No, you don't. If there's only room for one, then you need to be the most rested. I'll take the floor," Andy told him without hesitation.

Walker stared at the mattress longingly and agreed. "We can both fit if we sleep like we did last night." Then mumbled, "If I can get to sleep at all."

"I'm not ignorant to the problems our sleeping next to each other probably causes you, but you've proven to be a gentleman. I'll ignore your natural response to me if you acknowledge it's simply proximity and nothing more."

It took Walker a moment after lying down behind Andy to realize what she had actually said. He was tired and had become dazed when she began talking about sleeping next to one another, but she basically had told him she knew he had an erection sleeping next to her. This woman was making him reassess his ideas about everything he thought he knew. She was fearless, sensible and anything but squeamish.

What was he supposed to think about a young woman like Andy when she spoke about things most young women didn't or, at least, pretended not to know about? She was so forthright and honest she blurted out the first thing that came into her mind. He had to admire her ability to face the world honestly, that was for sure.

He would be sorry when they got to the cattle town where his boss was waiting for him. With his job, meeting up with Andy again after leaving her with the local sheriff would be difficult if not impossible. All he knew of her was her name and that she was going to Lemmoxville to be with her sister. Did she have parents, too? Did she live in a town he passed near? He wanted to know more about Andy, but he needed to get some sleep right now.

Walker kept himself a little away from Andy, well as much as he could considering they were two adults sharing a cot. Soon little snores were coming from Andy and he relaxed, allowing the parts of his body to touch her that were going to touch her. His contented even breathing took the place of his worries.

Andy stopped pretending to snore and relaxed. She liked the weight of Walker's arm over her, cuddling her body closer to his. She was going to be sorry when they reached a town where she could catch a coach back to Lemmoxville. She only knew his name and with a job like he had, she knew he travelled the state following leads in all sorts of criminal cases.

And she knew her sisters would never allow her to become involved with a lawman, even one as innocuous as Walker seemed. She would need to remember their vow and stick to their plans. When she fell asleep, she was hoping she wouldn't really snore like her sister always teased her of doing.

Andy blinked as the sun's muted rays caused the sky to turn from pink to yellow. Walker had told her to wait in the jail while he went to get his horse and bring it across the street to the back of the building. She would need to wait to relieve herself. Walker was unwilling for anyone in town to see who he was travelling with on a single horse. He knew they could be easily over-run if someone took a fancy of abducting her.

They were a little over a mile from town when Walker stopped and helped Andy dismount to take care of the necessary. Then he took time to check the bedroll and the refilled canteen. The horse seemed fresher after a warm night and grain in the livery and even though the people were hungry, they both were more rested then the morning before. How much a mattress and roof over one's head can change a person's perspective.

"I'm hoping we'll meet up with my partner tonight. Either way, you should be in a clean, warm bed when you wake-up tomorrow morning," Walker rashly promised Andy as if he'd been reading her thoughts.

"That would be nice, possibly some hot food, too?" she added to the dream.

"Yeah, maybe some hot food, too," he said and they both got back onto the horse for their long day in the saddle.

It had not been an empty promise. The two tired people and one heroically tired horse walked into the town that was a lot cleaner and safer than the last one they visited. Walker went to the jail first but found it empty so went over to the saloon, the second place his partner would be this time of night.

Walker walked in, Andy behind him, but he knew this saloon and it wasn't like the last one at all. This was a casino and not just a plain old bar. There were working girls, of course. What right minded proprietor wouldn't furnish his patrons with everything they wanted so they didn't leave the tables, well not for long, to get what they desired?

The casino with its highly-polished wood everywhere - bar, tables and chairs, as well as, the gaming equipment appeared prosperous and inviting. The wheel of fortune and the roulette table were being run by decorative ladies dressed in evening gowns, their bare shoulders and tantalizing amounts of flesh above the top of their dresses making it difficult for a man to care whether he lost his money or, at least, not to her.

That's where he found his partner, the marshal. He was talking with a tall red-haired beauty running the roulette table, but Walker knew Devlin wasn't betting on the game of chance himself. The woman was outstanding, though. Tall and willowy and porcelain skinned. Red hair but natural, not out of a henna bottle. Green eyes glittering with anger or was it passion as she kept the game going and parlayed verbally with the marshal. The green dress did something for her body, Walker wasn't sure what, but he was sure his friend and boss knew.

There was something familiar about the woman, but he didn't have time to analyze her right now. He had to report to the marshal so he could concentrate on taking care of Andy.

"This way," he said heading toward the marshal, hearing a little squeak behind him as Andy followed. Then there was a blur of gray as Andy ran past him and threw herself into the redheaded Amazon's arms sobbing, the tears streaming down her face.

The irate woman hugged Andy to her and turned on Walker. Her green eyes furious as she screamed accusingly, "What have you done to my baby sister?"

Before Walker could explain, the marshal turned on his friend and partner just as angrily, already judging and finding Walker guilty.

CHAPTER THREE

Devlin focused on Walker and barked, "What the hell, Walker. What were you thinking travelling with a young girl like this? Damn! All I asked is that you get your ass over here. No one told you to stop and pick-up an innocent and traumatize her."

Walker seemed confused still trying to figure out what was happening when a round little man with a patch of long hair combed to cover his balding pate hurried over and said excitedly, his French accent heavy with worry.

"This must stop. You are causing everyone to quit the games and all are watching you, like some kind of drama unfolding."

"May I use the private office, Maurice?" Ginger asked, the first to start thinking rationally now that she knew her little sister wasn't physically or sexually harmed.

"Yes, yes, of course, or we shall never get the games going again." Her boss smiled widely and then to the room, calmly explained, "Merely a little family squabble, gentlemen. Let them settle things among themselves. Ladies, pass out complimentary champagne for all our guests." He waved his hands in the air urging the ladies strolling about between customers to do his bidding.

By the time all four were in the office, Andy was down to hiccupping sobs as Ginger was talking quietly in her ear, the men unable to hear anything that was being said.

Devlin glared at Walker expecting an answer to make all this clear, but Walker just returned a look of blank fear.

"I didn't do anything. I picked her up after the stage got robbed. She was the only one left alive. I couldn't take her on to Lemmoxville, in case the bushwhackers went that direction. I had to bring her with me. She never said her sister was here. Just that she was to meet her at the coach line in Lemmoxville. I swear I did my best to keep her safe. I wanted to do a lot of things, but I didn't do any of them," Walker told his superior honestly.

Devlin was disgusted. "All right, here's a key. I'm in room twenty-four at the hotel just a few doors down. Get yourself a bath and cleaned up. Take one of my shirts if you don't have any clean ones. Don't come back here. I'll clean up this mess."

Walker hesitated, watching Andy, still confused and wondering what happened to the stalwart travelling companion of just half an hour ago.

Turning to Ginger, Devlin asked worriedly, "Is she all right? Is she hurt?"

Ginger turned eyes filled with unshed tears and shook her head, unable to speak. She kept shushing the small slight girl, who seemed to be about sixteen, petting her hair and murmuring little nonsense words into her ear, calming her into fewer and fewer sobs.

Finally holding Andy close to her side, Ginger explained, "She's been holding it all in since the coach was over turned. She saw four men killed in front of her and a horse shot in the head. Then she had to pull the dead bodies into a pile to keep the vultures from getting them. That was over two days ago, and she's slept very little and had about as much food. I think your deputy did what he could, and I think I appreciate what he did for Andy, but I'm taking her back to my room. Please leave us alone to recover."

"I'll go with you. Make sure you get there unmolested," Walker told them. "I promised to get Andy to a safe place and want to be sure she does."

Unless he wanted Ginger to think he was a complete brute, the only thing Devlin could do was agree. This young girl wasn't going to be much of a witness right now. She was visibly traumatized so this was probably the best plan. He'd need to get more information from Walker if there was any.

Devlin debriefed Walker, getting all the facts from that man. He waited till a decent time in the morning to speak with Ginger so he could question the sister. According to Walker, she had a lot of information on the individual men involved in the stage robbery.

He went to the door of Ginger's room. There was no answer so he went down to the dining room thinking she was feeding the girl, but that room was empty except for an older couple and a businessman reading the paper with his pot of coffee.

When he went to the front desk to ask about Ginger's whereabouts, he was told by the apologetic clerk she had checked-out and left with her bags earlier that morning.

Devlin swore and turned, almost running in his haste to the closed, empty casino and burst in, spotting Maurice having his late breakfast at a corner table.

"Where is she?" Devlin snarled at the man.

"She? Oh, you mean, Ginger. Because of you, I am short a dealer and she was the best draw I had. My clients doubled after she came to work for me. It will be all your fault if I do not make a profit now," the little man said pouting.

"So, you know she's gone. Did she say where she was going?" he asked less frantically knowing she probably left on the early train.

"No, she came by already dressed to travel. Lovely she was, with a pretty little hat perched up on top of…" His description was interrupted by another snarl from his audience.

"I don't want a fashion report. I want to know where she was heading besides the way the train was going!" Devlin said between clenched teeth.

"I was telling you. She didn't say. Just asked for her wages and the money I was holding in the safe for her. Previous earnings, savings of a sort. It was quite a lot for her being here such a short time. The men really liked her, gave very generously they did," he told the now irate Devlin.

"I don't want to hear that. She was a lady and I treated her as less. My own damn fault for her running, I guess. Now I'll have to figure out where she ran to. What other casinos would hire her?" he asked the little man.

"Why, you've seen her. Any casino manager would be glad to have her even if she does limit her charms to the casino floor only. There are enough women that can take care of a man's needs, but Ginger has special skills," the man said confidentially.

"What the hell are you talking about, Maurice? I'm going to start beating you if you don't start talking to me in plain English. I know you know how. You're from Brooklyn for God's sake."

Without a trace of the faux French accent Maurice or whatever his name really was, said, "Take it easy, Devil. If she wouldn't go to bed with you, what chance do you think the rest of us had? She didn't allow anything like that. She told me up front she wouldn't entertain the men in anyway other than to allow them to think they had a chance. She dressed like a duchess, spoke like a real lady and could drink any man under the table if she wanted."

"More, tell me more about her skills," Devlin asked bluntly.

"Besides being able to drink a man under the table, which I consider a skill by the way, she could see a card shark coming a mile away. I tested her out." At the darkening of Devil's eyes, Maurice quickly explained, "With cheating tricks. I tried to fool her, tried every way to stack the deck, add cards, take away cards, and deal from the top, bottom and middle. She caught me every time and I'm not bragging when I say I'm very good at those things. Then she sat down and taught me a few new tricks. I hired her immediately, paying her what my top man is paid and I felt I got my money's worth." Maurice finally came to a finish.

"So, you never felt she was palming chips or coins? Never felt she cheated anyone?" Devlin asked still trying to figure out why Ginger kept moving on. Maybe it happened when a man got too close, like he had.

"Never, I often left her counting the boxes and bundling the cash. I never doubted her honesty, just loyalty. I knew she'd move on. She was always hunting for someone. I think it's a man. Sometimes she would question the gamblers from out of town. I couldn't put my finger on it but then again, I wasn't trying. I was lucky she stopped off in this small-time town as it is. She sure was a beauty though," Maurice said with a faraway look in his eyes like he was remembering the redheaded siren.

Devil, never too delicate a speaker said, "I thought you leaned in a completely different direction."

Maurice laughed, not offended in the least, saying, "Men who are already losing their money, don't want to think they have competition for the women in the room too, at least not from the house. Anyway, she didn't pay me any attention. That was one woman I would have broken my own rules with, but I'm sure you agree with me. If I were a betting man, I'd bet you're asking these questions more to find her for yourself than for any other reason."

"Go screw yourself, Maurice," Devlin bit out as he turned and left to pack his own bag as the other man's laughter followed him out of the casino. He had a train to catch.

CHAPTER FOUR

Pacing back and forth in front of the Pinkerton Detective Agency's office, the pretty, blond young lady chewed a hole in the finger of one of her gloves. She was dressed nicely, the stylish bustle swaying delectably as she took each step then turned and retraced her path. The high brimmed hat framed her oval face with wide blue eyes and bow shaped mouth being monopolized by the now torn glove.

Preston George watched the young lady first with idle curiosity and then male interest. Putting on his hat, he waved goodbye to the man at the desk and went down the steps to the sidewalk where the indecisive young woman still paced.

"Miss?" He approached the blond and she stopped, large blue eyes focused on him, almost making him forget the casual remark he was going to make. He finally remembered to say something and finished with, "You seem worried. I'm a Pinkerton agent, Preston George. Can I be of service?"

"I have a missing sister, but I don't have the funds to hire your firm. It's just that she was due in on the stage and no one will tell me anything." Her eyes began to fill with tears.

Preston realized he was now in the middle of the street with a pretty blond in tears, and what his cohorts would deduce and tease him about he hated to think.

"Please come this way, Miss." He coaxed taking her to the cozy coffee shop around the corner that the agents tended to use throughout the day. Thankfully all the other agents seemed to be on assignment that kept them busy elsewhere.

The waiter acknowledged Preston's nod of his head and brought his regular order and a tea for his companion. Preston sat the lady down and then said again, "Tell me more of this missing sister."

"Well, she's actually my twin, not identical, but twin none-the-less. She hurt her ankle and had to stay in the last place we were living until she could travel while I came on ahead. I had a job waiting, but it wouldn't wait, if you understand." She smiled sweetly. "I know this is sounding complicated and you are being so kind to take the time to listen to me."

"You would have lost the job if you hadn't come when you did." Preston stated for her.

"Exactly. I didn't dare miss out since jobs are too difficult for an unmarried lady to find," she said, underlining to Preston she was indeed free of male encumbrances. What man would allow such a beautiful lady as this one to move to another city? She hadn't been here long enough to form any kind of attachment yet, he could tell.

"Do you mind if I ask your name and that of the missing sister?" he said getting out the small pad of paper and pencil all Pinkerton agents carried.

The young lady smiled and said with confidence, "I'm, Meg Wheeler, and my sister is, Miranda Wheeler. She was to travel on the Bentley Coach Line out of Taxco to Lemmoxville and she should have gotten in yesterday, early afternoon. But when she didn't show up, when a coach didn't even arrive, no one in their offices would speak with me about it."

Preston sat straighter when Meg mentioned the coach line. As a trained professional he didn't let her know he knew of the coach line and that two of their agents had been shot in an ambush and everyone else killed. The other main problem, of course, was that although a six-man posse and four Pinkerton agents had been out to the site, no one reported seeing any sign of a young lady of any age.

Slowly he asked again, "You're sure your sister was on that coach?"

She took out a folded Western Union telegraph message. "I received this the day before. At the same time, she would have gotten on the coach. It states very plainly the time she expected to arrive and that I should meet her since she didn't have my address, yet."

Preston read over the few words on the message and agreed, "Yes, I see that is what it says." Then he gazed into those lovely blue eyes, sparkling with unshed tears and promised a promise he hoped to hell he wasn't going to be sorry he made. "I promise to find her for you, no charge. A single woman should be able to travel safely on public transportation."

"Oh, thank you, sir, I mean, Mr. George. This means so much to me, and I cannot feel right until we are together again. We have never been apart before and I felt so guilty leaving her in the first place, but she insisted. I don't know what I would have done if you hadn't come to my aid," she said, the gratitude openly on her face.

Embarrassed at the, as yet, unearned appreciation, Preston got Meg's address and said it may take him a couple of days to check out everything. He told her he would pass on any information each night if she would meet him at the coffee shop at six o'clock.

Meg was very punctual and met Preston the two nights and then on the third day Meg came in all excited to tell him her twin had been found, alive and unharmed.

Meg went on to explain, "After having her trunk placed on the coach, Miranda feared getting sick on the long ride so didn't board the coach after all. Instead, she took the longer train trip to our older sister, Beatrice. Beatrice then accompanied Miranda to Lemmoxville and everything is fine now. They arrived this morning by train."

Preston was relieved because he had begun to fall in love with the pretty, sensitive Meg and didn't want to be the one to tell her robbers may have carried her twin off, and that she may never see her again. He hadn't wanted to add that a pretty, white female was worth money across the border and that the stage robbers could have abused her themselves before selling her off. Preston felt Miranda was a very lucky young lady to have changed her mind on taking the stage and Preston was a very lucky man to have found Meg.

"Please, may I bring my sisters to meet you so they can add their gratitude to mine? They are very appreciative of the fact you were willing to help me even though I didn't have the funds to pay you for your efforts." She smiled up at him prettily.

Preston met Meg's two other sisters so they could add their grateful thanks to hers. He thought they were all lovely, well-bred young ladies of quality who had been brought low after the death of their father. Beatrice, the oldest, kept the family together as best she could. The twins, though young, helped with the family finances by taking jobs.

He didn't care much for the fact Meg had gotten a position somehow in a casino. That was why he was there to watch over her every evening. Why he had a talk with the manager about protecting Meg whenever Preston was on a job elsewhere. He stayed out of the customer's way and, of course, no one knew he was a Pinkerton except her employer. But the patrons knew she was under his protection and none of them bothered her more than once.

CHAPTER FIVE

The train pulled into Lemmoxville and Devlin grabbed his bag as Walker swung down from the train car unto the heavily trafficked wood platform carrying his saddlebags.

"Where to from here, Marshal?" asked Walker. Devlin knew the younger man was eager to see this Andy again.

"I thought I'd check the gambling places, and you can check the surrounding boarding houses for anyone fitting their descriptions. And remember, they may approach a landlady alone, not as two sisters," Devlin warned Walker remembering that Ginger had been moving from town to town either running from someone or to someone. Devlin hated to think it was a man as Maurice suspected.

"I'll work from descriptions, but a lot of these places won't take single women. I can rule those out quick enough. Meet up at the sheriff's office at dusk?" Walker asked.

"Then we'll grab a bite and visit the rest of the gambling dens I haven't gotten to, although it may be too soon for her to have secured a job. I think Ginger had this plan in mind before we showed up there. After all, this is where Andy was supposed to end up before the stage got robbed. It's the most efficient route from the south-east." Devlin flagged down a cab to take him into the commercial district.

Walker arrived at the town's sheriff's office before Devlin, the streetlights being lit as he sat waiting impatiently. Maybe Devlin's absence meant he found them. He threw out that idea knowing there would have been a message waiting for Walker at the office if that were the case. But the sheriff knew nothing, just that the two federal lawmen were hunting for two fugitives. Walker didn't enlighten that fine gentlemen to the truth that the women weren't actual fugitives, that one was only a witness wanted for questioning.

Devlin came up the street. "I left our bags at a small hotel nearby and a second room is already secured for you. At the down-in-the-mouth look of you, there wasn't any luck?"

Walker shook his head. "But there's a lot of boarding houses and rooms to let. Maybe tomorrow. I knew it wouldn't be easy in a town this size."

"I found a restaurant near the hotel that would be a good place for a meal. It has wide windows to the street so, you never know, we may get lucky and spot them."

The two men began to think there wasn't anything like luck for them at all. At least, they had been given the assignment of capturing the stagecoach robbers since men had been killed. That would keep them in Lemmoxville for a while. Finding Andy and the possible information she had became more urgent. She was the only one with firsthand knowledge of what the horses and men looked like and Walker was sure she would be able to tell them down to the weight, if given enough time.

After several days, the two lawmen walked into a small gaming house off a side street that catered to high-stakes poker games and found the manager, Mr. Thomas, at the door greeting his customers.

Devlin began with his usual first question, "I was wondering if you've hired a new female dealer lately."

The manager focused on the two men, both wearing

badges and said cautiously, "Why do you want to know?"

"Just seeking a witness to a crime. We don't want to take her into custody or anything," Devlin said, his heart beating erratically knowing they may be close to finding Ginger.

The manager relaxed a little. "Good, because I noticed the men at her table tend to stay longer and play deeper trying to impress her. I certainly don't want to lose her so soon. She's one of those women who are easy on the eyes, her body makes promises and her mind is quick as a whip. Nothing gets past her. No cheaters are allowed to ply their trade here anymore."

With that description, Devlin's heartbeat went into double-time. This description had to be Ginger no matter what name she may be using to hide from him.

"Yeah, she's right over there at the main Black Jack table. I can give her a break if you need to speak with her but I can't spare her for long or the table will clear out." He smiled, letting them know he knew how priceless his dealer was to the casino.

Devlin and Walker both eagerly turned toward the direction the manager pointed to be disappointed when they saw a pretty petit blond. Her blue eyes flashed with amusement as she chatted with the men at her table and dealt out cards, asking for bets then clearing the winnings for the house. She was dressed in a dark blue gown, brocade with velvet trim but the décolletage was cut low and her ample breasts were main focus-points for the players.

He watched the way she dealt the cards and cleared the table, remembering other soft hands, the same porcelain skin, the same arched brows and slightly wide-set eyes.

"Damn, there are three of them. Well, at least three. This has to be a sister to Ginger and Andy or I'll eat my hat." Devlin swore and his eyes fixed hungrily on the blond as he became surer and surer watching her, the trill of her laughter, the peeking up through her lashes, all to flirt a promise that was accepted but never made. Oh, yes, this little vixen was part of the matriarchal den.

"Mr. Thomas, I think I'd like to speak with this young woman in a quiet place if I may. I promise I won't take her for long. You can assure the gentlemen at her table she will return to them soon." He offered the manager the promise in lieu of any real consideration.

The manager knew he was out-played. Two of a kind to his single Ace and the badges won every time. "I can let you use the office up front here. I'll bring Meg to you."

Devlin, knowing how slippery these women could be, said, "No, we'll get her ourselves. You should be taking care of your customers."

Both Walker and Devlin approached the table, his gaze searching for any backdoor the young woman might escape through. As they almost reached the table an acquaintance they both knew intervened.

"Devlin, Walker, what has you in my neck of the woods? Get tired of herding up rustlers?" teased the man just slightly shorter than Devlin, with light brown hair and clear gray eyes trained to detect the slightest nuances.

"Preston, you stationed here, then? I hadn't heard. We're here on that stagecoach robbery from last week. I know you lost a couple of good men, sorry to hear that." Devlin said conveying his condolences to the Pinkerton

43

agency.

"I have a personal interest in that case. Mind telling me what you're here for?" the attractive man wearing a gray, wool suit and black tie asked.

"Following up a lead to an eye witness," Devlin said watching the blonde's eyes as she measured the distance between herself and the rear door, which had a burly bouncer watching it.

"I can assure you the young woman you are approaching knows nothing of the incident. She was here in town. I know that, for a fact," Preston said honestly telling the other two lawmen the truth as he knew it.

"It's not her we're interested in. It's her sister," Walker finally added to the conversation. "We're anxious to speak with this sister to find Andy, protect her if we need to." Devlin knew his friend wasn't searching for a witness but to ensure Andy was safe.

"No, that turned out to be a mistake, too. Meg's sister was supposed to be on that coach, but luckily she changed her mind and met up with the older sister, Beatrice, and came in by train instead." Preston informed them, again thinking he was imparting the truth.

Devlin looked almost sadly at Preston, knowing the man was going to feel a fool letting three young women pull the wool over his eyes and then swearing to two lawmen it was the gospel.

Just as Devlin was going to tell Preston to step back so he could get to this Meg, the young lady in question threw the cards onto the table and darted to the rear door yelling she was going to be sick and that the guard better open the door for her quickly.

The guard got up, swiftly unlocked the door, throwing it open for the young lady before she embarrassed herself completely in front of the casino patrons. Devlin and Walker were right behind her, but the guard tried to stop them before he saw their badges. Then, apologizing let them through, also. Preston called out for Meg to stop, but then he disappeared.

Outside, the two lawmen glanced one way then the other and found it to be a dead end so ran towards the street and the front of the casino. Once there, they found Preston holding a distraught Meg as he tried to calm her, whispering into her ear that the two men chasing her wouldn't hurt her, that he wouldn't let them hurt her.

Devlin and Walker, both trying to catch their breaths from the sprint, looked at each other and they both thought, but Devlin said, "Damn, another one hits the skids. These women are a danger to society with their big innocent eyes and the butter wouldn't melt in their mouth smiles. I don't know if we have a chance if we ever get them all in one room."

Meg finally stopped trembling and Preston told the two men, "I can't let you talk to her now. She's too fragile. You'll need to talk to Beatrice. She'll be able to tell you what you want to know, I'm sure."

Devlin heard Meg beg Preston, "Please, don't leave me with them. Don't tell them where we're living if you have any feelings for me at all. Don't let them get the others."

Devlin was saying, almost hurting for what the Pinkerton was going to go through when he learned the truth, "Preston, I know I don't have to tell you where your duty lies. I understand you're torn but she's not worth your career."

"Maybe I think she is," said Preston, holding Meg up against his chest, trying to keep her warm as well as protect her from Devlin and Walker.

"Let's go back in. Thomas said we could use the office up front here and ah, Meg, will be warmer inside," Devil said, hoping Preston wasn't going to pull a gun on them or some fool thing to save his ladylove.

The foursome went into the private area, the casino gaming floor just getting back to normal play. All except Meg's table, which was still in a mild up-roar.

"Meg, I can't tell if these tears are real or not but if you keep Preston from working with us, he'll lose his job. Maybe even go to prison for interfering with a law officer's duties," Devlin said sitting next to the still frightened girl.

Meg tipped her head and peered out from Preston's embrace, real fear showing. "I'm not to tell. Beatrice is protecting, Miranda. Men will kill Miranda if they know where she's at."

"We're not those men, we're seeking those men, too. Deputy Walker here helped Andy, ah, Miranda, when the coach over-turned. He returned her to Ginger, no, she must be Beatrice."

Pushing herself away from Preston, Meg asked gazing at the younger man, "You're Walker? Andy said you were kind, the very epitome of a gentleman."

Walker's ears turn red, receiving a compliment via a possible suspect in a crime wasn't something one wanted to happen, especially in his superior's hearing. "I was just doing my duty, Miss. I had to go to the marshal and I had to take Andy, ah, Miss Taylor with me."

"Wait, who's Miss Taylor? I'm getting confused," Preston complained, still not releasing Meg completely.

"It wouldn't be so confusing if we had everyone's correct name. In fact, it would cut the number of players in this theatrical drama in half, maybe more," Devlin said, taking off his hat and rubbing his hand through his hair.

"Preston," Devlin barked out the Pinkerton's name, "Do you know where the three young ladies reside?"

"Yes, they are all staying in the rooms that Meg rented," he answered which wasn't an answer at all.

"Meg, is that your real name?" As Preston blustered his outrage at Devlin calling Meg a liar, he became quiet when that young lady shook her head as tears rolled down her cheeks again.

"Let's start there then. Telling us your real name won't hurt Andy. I take it that's the real name for the sister that was at the stagecoach robbery?" Devlin tried something easy.

Meg, or whoever, shook her head again and large tears dropped off her chin unto Preston's starched white shirt.

"Christ, we don't even know the players!" Devlin swore which had Meg burying her head in Preston's chest again, bringing out all sorts of protectiveness from that man.

"This isn't working, Devlin. You're scaring her out of her wits," Walker said, deciding he was better at talking to these women.

At that name, the pseudo Meg, stared wide-eyed at Devlin and accused, "You're the Devil. We wouldn't be in danger now if it weren't for you. Beatrice said it was all your fault."

All three glared at him as if he were the devil.

"All right, but Andy and I got along quite well. Andy is a nick-name, one you sisters use correct?" Walker asked and was rewarded with a nod of her head.

Walker gave a 'that's how it's done' look at Devlin who scowled at Walker's small victory.

"And Beatrice has beautiful red hair and amazing green eyes, right?" Walker described Ginger as Devlin scowled even deeper showing his displeasure that Walker found Ginger's hair beautiful and her eyes amazing.

But once again, Meg nodded in agreement her tears drying on her face and no new ones forming.

"Now we all know Meg isn't your name so why don't you tell us your real name?" Walker asked.

Peeking worriedly at Preston the young girl almost whispered, "Trudy, it's short for Gertrude. I'm afraid none of us like our names since we were all named after dead aunts our mother was quite devoted to."

Walker said honestly, hoping Trudy could see how sincere he was, "Now I became very fond, I mean really very fond, of Andy. I want to speak with her, make sure she's still all right, still able to handle what happened to her, what she went through."

"I think she grew, umm, fond of you, too. She hoped to see you again someday and thank you personally for saving her and to apologize for leaving you in the lurch," Trudy said, the longest sentence spoken to anyone besides Preston.

"All right, Preston is going to take you home and he's going to ask Beatrice and Andy to meet us at a little restaurant, neutral ground. Does that meet with your approval?" Walker asked politely, disregarding Devlin's snort of impatience.

Ignoring everything else, Walker told Preston the ladies could name the day and time but speed was of an essence. Getting these men's description out there would go a long way to capturing them before they moved on to another state or country, which is what they've been doing for the past year. Once that happens even Federal officers wouldn't be able reach them.

Walker had already given the authorities what Andy told him right after the attack, but Walker was sure she was remembering more as they had travelled.

"I'm afraid I'm going to lose my job and we need this money. It's the most any of us make and we need it to keep, um, we need it for dresses and things," Trudy fabricated, but none of the men called her on it. Some things they would need to wait to learn.

"I'll speak to the manger for you, but I think it will be all right. I have a feeling he knows how valuable you are as a dealer," Devlin said, finally relaxing enough to be friendly now that seeing Ginger was becoming a reality. He met Walker's gaze and ignored the couple as Preston wiped the girl's eyes and spoke quietly with her.

CHAPTER SIX

Devlin and Walker, both wearing suits with white starched shirts and black ties, their boots polished and their hats freshly blocked, waited outside the restaurant. They planned to walk in as a group, like two couples dining out together, so as not to attract attention.

Preston brought Andy who was wearing a day dress with flounces around the hemline, lace trim at the tight wrists and a crocheted collar. It was topped by a cape with hood that could cover her hair, which was wrapped into a large figure eight at the back of her head. Walker went to her immediately, smiling and taking her hand, making a connection with her that he had missed.

"Where's Ging... Beatrice? Why isn't she with you," Devlin asked impatiently.

"Bea got held-over at work. Her replacement didn't show, but she said she'll try to get here as soon as possible," Andy told them both as Preston excused himself to go back to Trudy who was still working at the casino this time of night.

"Where is she? I don't want her walking the streets after dark alone," Devlin said worriedly.

Walker nodded to Andy to tell Devlin. "He can be trusted not to let anyone harm Beatrice." She told him the street address and Devlin took off at a run.

"Let's go inside and wait at our table. We can order a drink to get you warmer. Your hands are freezing even in these gloves," Walker said as he led her inside.

Devlin cut through a couple of alleys, knowing this city from previous cases, to reach his destination. He didn't see Ginger, no, he must stop thinking of her in that manner. Bea, he didn't see, Bea. Peering through the steam covered window, he saw her wearing a simple dress of some striped material and a bibbed apron making her appear taller and even slimmer.

Although, maybe she had lost weight, he thought, as he remembered her eating only one meal a day before when she was bringing in good money. Now there were three of them and being a waitress couldn't pay much in a restaurant such as this. Clean but the meals were priced to attract the workingman, not someone who ordered a' la carte and left large gratuities. Meals here were over by seven o'clock, not just beginning as they were in hotel restaurants where male waiters were de rigueur.

He felt guilty knowing she could have still been working at the casino, making high wages and getting lucrative gifts from the customers. He ground his teeth merely thinking of those men staring at her, wanting to touch her, lusting after her like dogs after a bitch in heat. Then he remembered he had been at the head of the pack, even Maurice had backed off.

Hell, who was he trying to fool. Both Walker and Preston by now knew that Gin, Bea, didn't have any connection to this case. This had become personal because when she ran, she hadn't just run from the law, she had run from him. She was afraid of him.

Devlin pushed open the door and a little chime rang out to announce a new customer.

A male voice called from the back of the building, "We're closed. We're just finishing with the last customers, but the stove's cooled down and we're cleaning up."

"All right, I'll come back another time," Devlin answered but he knew Bea had seen him and she hadn't turned away or tried to run. Both good signs to Devlin's way of thinking.

A few minutes later the last customer left the restaurant huddled into his coat, heading for home. Then he saw Bea come out, wearing a gray cape over her striped dress and he walked up to her.

"I don't have time to change so this will have to do," she said in way of an apology.

He studied her, eating her up with his eyes, which made her blush and lower her head. "Don't hide from me, Red. You don't ever have to hide from me again. Whatever you need, wherever you go, let me in. Let me help you. I've hated every minute I didn't know where you were, wondering if you were safe, if you were eating."

"Red? That's what you're going to stay with?" she laughed at the absurd nickname.

"Well, I liked Ginger, but it seems it's a persona that you've shed. Red you're kind of stuck with." He glanced at the much less elaborate hairstyle then she wore for the casino job. All the rest, the amazing green eyes, the cherry-pink bow shaped mouth, all the rest was pure…her. Devlin smiled for the first time in days, grateful he'd found the woman he once thought lost to him.

"Come on, Walker will have ordered and eaten all the food if we don't get there soon," he urged as he placed her arm in the crook of his and hurried her along the paved brick sidewalks.

Once Devlin and Bea arrived, the waiter promptly took everyone's order and left them to talk.

Walker poured coffee for Bea and Devlin. Then told Devlin, "Andy gave me a more complete description of the men and their horses although nothing that would make finding them easier. She also mentioned the Indian items that were incongruent with any tribe in the area let alone a raiding party."

This information would be added to the information the posse and Pinkertons found after the robbery, where the trail died out along with anything of note.

"This is strictly for our ears only. We won't have Andy come in and swear out anything. No one will know her name or where she's living. She used Miranda Taylor as the name for the ticket, but that's not what they're using now," Walker told Devlin in confidence.

Devlin watched Red, trying to get enough of her so he would be content to stay in his hotel and leave her alone in the rooms she was renting with her sisters. "What last name, Red? Anything beginning with an O?" he teased.

Andy glanced toward her older sister who smiled saying, "No. It's Wheeler. Nothing sinister or memorable in that name."

"Wheeler, it is. Good to know. At least this time I'll have a starting place," Devlin said. "Why did you give up the casino work and have Trudy do it?"

Bea appeared guilty and admitted, "I knew you would be searching for me, probably in this town because this is where Andy was headed when the stage got robbed. I didn't think you'd find Trudy out, though. She doesn't look like me or Andy."

"Well, it was…No, I won't tell you. I'm afraid you'll run again and change things so I won't be able to find you. As I said, you don't need to run from me," Devlin finished and would have taken her ungloved hand to his lips, but the waiter came with their meal and the talk changed to normal table conversation.

Walker and Devlin escorted the two sisters home. Both ladies said goodnight at the outside door stating the landlady had a strict rule about male guests in and around the premises, especially after dark. The men nodded their understanding and went back to their hotel in total dejection.

"Do you feel as shitty as I do?" asked Walker.

"Probably, but we're going to have to live with it. These are nice ladies even if they live a little unorthodoxly. They may need to make us honest men before we feel better about ourselves," Devlin told his friend. He knew he cringed inside even thinking such a thing.

Walker seemed to think it over. "You know, a few weeks ago, that statement would have had me running for the hills, but now it's sort of attractive."

"To me, too," agreed Devlin morosely, climbing the stairs to their rooms.

With everyone knowing about the three sisters, everyone that could make for a disaster at least, Bea went to work for a competing casino to increase the family's finances. She saved most of her wages and gifts, keeping them in a secret drawer in the top of their traveling trunks. It wasn't the safest place, but she felt she needed to have the funds available if the family had to move quickly again.

Bea needed to be in the casino world to do what she needed to do. Devlin wasn't pleased with her going to work there, but then again, he didn't like to see her working so hard in the restaurant for such low wages, either. Besides, what Devlin wanted didn't go very far with Bea's plans.

She found Devlin hanging around the casino where

she worked, his badge in plain sight, so he could walk her home. He was putting a crimp in Bea's ability to get information from the customers because Devlin couldn't have been clearer with his message: *Look but don't touch, and oh, yeah, I was kidding about the look part, too.*

Bea knew she would need to stop both Preston and Devlin from watching over the Wheeler sisters while they were at work. Trudy wasn't happy about the situation but agreed the men were getting in the way of their real business at hand.

Devlin was the first to leave. It wasn't easy and it wasn't pretty.

"Devlin, I won't need you to walk me home tonight so I'd appreciate your leaving early," Bea, using the name of Ginger again in her work place, told him part way through the evening.

"I've told you before, this town isn't really safe for women at night," he told her firmly. She could tell he was trying to figure out why she was bringing-up this topic again after he thought it was settled.

One of the newer dealers came up behind Bea and placed several decks of unopened cards in front of her, brushing her arm as he did. The movement earned him a dirty look from Devlin, but a smile of appreciation from Bea that had the man smiling widely and ignoring Devlin's glare.

"I know, but I have an escort who will walk me home when we get done here without affecting his daytime job. Henry has offered since we are on the same shift and he lives not too far from my rooms," she explained quietly to Devlin.

"What about going out to dinner with me and

Walker and Andy?" He seemed to be testing his theory Bea was trying to push him out of her life.

"I don't think that's such a good idea, Devlin. I appreciate what Walker did for Andy, but we can't expect you two to watch over us forever. There's nothing linking us to the stage robbery and I can't see anyone trying to keep Andy from talking when she doesn't have anything to say."

Then with more emphasis added. "I have a life Devlin, and you're getting in the way. This job gives me the opportunity to meet rich men and you hanging around me makes that difficult. I need my freedom. I can't put it any blunter than that."

Bea stared him straight in the eye and urged him to move on, to leave her in peace, even if it was a miserable peace. She lowered her gaze so she wouldn't need to witness his last time in her life.

Devlin fought down his instinct to claim her right then, brand her as his property, hobble her to keep her from roaming. Using any means but a wedding ring came into his mind. In the end, he bowed out of the picture admitting he didn't have what Bea evidently wanted or thought she wanted.

Walker and Andy sat at the table near the back of the restaurant, Walker facing the door and street, always the lawman even on his off hours.

"I'm being assigned to another town for a few days and then I'll be back. Don't do anything dangerous while I'm away," he teased to lessen his dread of leaving her alone.

"I don't do dangerous things, Walker. I read in the afternoon to an elderly lady and make a light meal for her before I leave. It doesn't pay much but she's sweet and lonely and I make a difference in her days, I think. I'll miss her." Then added quickly, "When she's gone. Her health isn't good and I'm only there to make her more comfortable."

"That's one of the things I find I like about you, Andy. You're so kindhearted. Even those scorpions in the dessert. You didn't think to kill them. Just move on until we were a safe distance from them," he said remembering their first night together.

"I'm not sure I wouldn't step on one in my living room, but we were in theirs, kind of, so we were the interlopers."

"I better get you home or Bea will have a fit. You're like her one lone chick only there's Trudy as well." He got up leaving the payment for the meal along with a hefty gratuity since they had monopolized the table for so long and were the last customers.

Part way home, Walker pulled Andy into the shelter of a corner garden and into his arms. His mouth covered hers as she turned her face up to his so he could take from her all she wanted to give.

"I really don't want to leave you. Not just tonight, but tomorrow, for so many days. I don't go a whole day without seeing you anymore." He kissed her soft cheek, her neck, her shell of an ear.

"Could I meet you at the station and say goodbye?" she asked quietly.

"No, I'll be out early. Five o'clock and Devlin will be with me. He wouldn't approve that I told you about the assignment at all," Walker confessed as he covered her mouth, sliding his tongue into the waiting warmth.

When they could speak again, Andy asked, "So

you'll be heading west?"

"No, we need to backtrack a little. Like I said, it shouldn't be long. Just following a trail that actually went cold, but we go where we're told to go." He hugged her to his warm body then took her arm in his and stepped back onto the sidewalk. They continued to her rooms where he tipped his hat to her as if they hadn't been wrapped around one another only moments earlier. She unlocked the door and entered the protection of her home.

Preston had Trudy pushed up against the wall of the empty backroom of the casino, everyone else was busy getting ready to go home for the night. This casino didn't stay open all day and night like some, just not enough money or too many casinos. Most of the men who frequented were businessmen working for their living so went home to sleep for a few hours before going in to an office in the downtown.

Preston, his mouth opening slightly to taste the warm, sweet skin as he brushed it over the expanse of flesh left available to him, moaned. "Please, Trudy, tell your sisters how much I mean to you. I swear I'll help them financially, but you've got to put me out of my misery. Marry me, Sweetheart. I can't keep seeing you here with other men ogling you. I nearly knocked a player out of his chair tonight." He returned to her lips not giving her time or air to respond.

Finally, she pushed him away as he realized what he was doing. "I'm sorry, Sweetheart, I'm behaving like an animal with you. It's just that I'm having a harder and harder time keeping my hands off you. I don't want you to think I don't respect you. I do. I treasure you and I want us to be together. I want the right to take care of you in every way. I'm asking again, will you marry me?"

Preston firmed his lips together, preventing himself from saying something that would offend Trudy or make her feel she must defend her sisters. But Bea was very controlling, probably due to having to take care of the twins for so long on her own. He knew the sisters loved one another and that family meant everything, but there came a time when each of them had to grow up, to become women and not only sisters. All this he thought but didn't dare say.

He was sure one day Trudy would tell her sisters she was in love with him and she'll come to him as his bride. Then the two of them would begin a whole new family and their children will have very attentive aunts.

"Let me get your cape. I better escort you home before my good intentions fly out the window. I'm thinking of taking up smoking. Walker says it takes the edge off the, ah, physical need. I'm ready to try anything," he confessed as he led her out the front door.

Trudy finally got some space between them and although it broke her heart, she owed her sisters so much more than she owed Preston and herself. Her wants would have to wait. "I'll try to bring it up the next time we're together. With Andy working days and Bea and I working evenings and sleeping late, there isn't much family time anymore." As his eyes darkened with desire again, she said quickly, "But I will bring it up. It just may take a couple of days."

Knowing she loved Preston and knowing she would be the one to hurt him more than anyone else in the world, Trudy hated the decision she needed to make. She didn't feel well, getting physically ill, deceiving this man who relied on the truth so much.

Bea walked alongside the burly man who was the bouncer at the casino, although not many customers got to the point of being tossed out of the gaming. It wasn't known for that kind of gaming being more sedate and a place for men of refined taste. Bea smiled and thanked the man in front of the house where she rented a room. She knew he was continuing home to his wife and three children.

She was almost to the door when she sniffed the air catching the scent of his cigarette and said, with a sigh, "You're not giving up are you, Devlin? I can't win."

"It's not like you'd be losing, Red. I've never had any complaints and I'm sure we'll be good together," he said without sounding like he was bragging.

There was a resigned smile on her face as she turned and came back down the steps accepting his arm. He walked with her the several blocks to his hotel, letting the silence surround them. She knew he didn't want to push his luck now that she had finally capitulated. They were going to be together as he desired, as a man and a woman were meant to be together.

Bea knew she wasn't being fair placing all the blame on Devlin for this. Curiosity about what he was talking about and her own attraction to the man was the main forces behind her accompanying him to his room. She had been interested in him from the start. Something about how he watched her, how he brushed against her at every chance, how he seemed to lean into her to smell her hair.

His fascination with her was a kind of aphrodisiac if she understood what the word meant. She had been acting in similar ways toward him. Her awareness of him as a male, a large, predatory male, was always present but she never felt in danger from his attentions. He had made it plain from the start he wanted her physically.

Besides, she had decided she was never going to have the happy husband and home she once dreamed of having, not after so many years on the road, so many cities in her past. She thought about what her sisters would say if they learned of this encounter, but knew they were too generous with their forgiveness and self-sacrifice themselves to begrudge her this night. They wouldn't reproach her any chance to know happiness or this time to learn what it was to be desired by a virile man who seemed to be fixated on her.

Devlin had made it clear he wanted Bea, no other woman was going to satisfy his need, not yet, anyway. Perhaps later, after he had bedded her. Then his eyes would once again wander to others, but Bea would make sure it wasn't to one of her sisters. They couldn't handle a man like Devlin and she never wanted them to get close enough to find that out.

She would accept what he was offering and then have something to look back on in her old age when she was bouncing her nephews and nieces on her knee, once she finally found Mick.

The couple entered the hotel and ascended the stairs without the desk clerk lifting his head from the book he was reading. Opening his door with the key, Devlin allowed Bea to enter first, all without a word passing between the two of them. Inspecting the room, she noted the large bed and side table, a desk and two chairs plus an armchair. There was a washstand and mirror near the window. The lamp was already lit, but the wick was turned low. Had he been expecting her to come back with him this evening? Was he so sure of her?

Bea turned to the quiet man behind her. "Now what?" Letting Devlin set the pace and steps to this unfamiliar dance.

"I take your cape and you remove your gloves and whatever you feel comfortable removing," he said with a smile, hanging the cape on a peg on the wall.

Bea stood there, not completely comfortable but not frightened of what she had decided to pursue. "I'm not sure what you expect of me," she said quietly.

Devlin smiled. "Let me help you. I've been dreaming of this for weeks. I'll try not to be clumsy in my eagerness."

He had already hung his coat and placed his hat on the table brim up then walked to where Bea was standing. Pulling her into his arms, he kissed her, their first kiss of this sort and Devlin didn't seem disappointed. Swooping in for more, he slid his tongue into her mouth, dueling with hers as they met and found one another.

Devlin pulled her hips to his. She enjoyed finally feeling her body next to his. Stroking his hand up her ribs, he cupped her breast as she felt the nipple respond through her corset.

"I need to feel you, all of you, Red," he growled as he turned her so he could unbutton the dress and let it slide to the floor. Untying the corset and her petticoat, he tossed them aside while kissing and sucking the nape of her neck. He kneeled, untying her stockings and rolling them down, raising each leg to kiss the calf and back of her knee. Placing his head between her legs to reach the sensitive spots. She felt her knees go weak and wondered why she had waited so long to experience this. She wanted to melt into this man and become one with him.

He stood fully dressed as she stood self-consciously in only her long camisole and then he pulled that unrestricted from her body. Carrying her to the turned down bed, he placed her on the cool sheets.

"You are the loveliest thing I've ever seen." Sitting on the bed, he leaned down to cover her breast with his chest, kissing her mouth and then her breasts, reveling in the freedom to touch her as he wanted. She offered herself up to his feasting.

"Just a moment." Reluctantly he left the naked Bea on the bed to remove his too many clothes tossing them toward the chair after tugging off his boots. He lay down beside her, his long legs next to hers, his hips within inches of that most sought place.

"Now we're even, Red. I can't believe this is finally going to happen for us." He kissed her lips but soon covered a waiting nipple, licking the tip to a peak and then suckling, first one than the other.

Writhing with the feelings his mouth caused, she felt relieved when his seeking hands kneaded her breasts. Devlin kissed his way over her stomach to the top of the mound covered with bright red curls.

"I knew I should call you Red for a reason," he chuckled and Bea felt his warm tongue seek access to her most private place.

Bea jumped and squeaked, but Devlin merely chuckled again. "Don't leave me. I'm doing this for both of us, believe me. Relax and let me enjoy you."

She wasn't sure what was happening but she liked it. His total concentration was on her and she soon realized there was a reason, a very, very interesting and impelling reason. Bea had her first orgasm with Devlin's mouth held tightly against her nub. He stayed there until all spasms clamored through her body.

Then he brought himself up even with her and like a homing pigeon, his highly-aroused erection found that same place his mouth just was and entered her swiftly.

Crying out in surprised pain, she covered her mouth as soon as the sound was released. Focused on the pain as it receded, she finally relaxed her body.

"Red, why didn't you tell me?" He kissed the tears sliding out from under closed lids.

"Why didn't you know?" she asked in return still hurting from the rough entry. All she could think was that he should have known or he thought her a wanton, loose with her body. Evidently, he did and the pain of that knowledge was like a knife piercing her heart.

Devlin tried to hold Bea afterwards, but she kept pulling away and then told him, "I need to be home, the twins will worry."

"I'm sorry I hurt you, Bea. It will be better next time, I swear." He tried to kiss her neck, get her to soften toward him, but it didn't happen.

Rising, she quickly dressed herself, ignoring Devlin as he re-dressed to walk her home.

The desk clerk didn't quite hide the smirk on his lips when she reached the foyer floor. *That's just great,* she thought, *that's all that was needed to make this evening perfect.* There were no more tears, it was done. She was a woman and she felt dead inside in spite of the most amazing thing happening to her. For the first time in her life, she felt she had chosen a path she should not have followed.

Neither one of them said a word on the walk back to her rooms, both thinking deeply.

Devlin was kicking himself for choosing this night of all nights to make love for the first time with Bea. Finding she was a virgin was plain dumb on his part for not making sure she knew what she was doing.

On top of that, the protection he had been so careful to procure was safely in its packet in the drawer next to his bed. But he had been so eager, so lost in his ability to give her pleasure…. It felt so perfect that he didn't even remember to pull one on.

Remembering their devastating joining, Devlin hadn't known how to make it better. He had felt the urge to finish, hoping he could bring Bea with him to a second culmination. But he was too primed and she was too disillusioned. Devlin couldn't tell if it were with him or herself. He didn't know which he wanted it to be either.

In her innocence, Bea didn't even question him about a condom. That should have been his first clue she didn't know enough to be anything but innocent. There were so many signs and he ignored them all because he was so sure of his instincts about people. What he did was look at her and thought she was what he concluded she was. Now how did he recover from this debacle? And on a night he was leaving town. He'd have to explain his absence.

Speeding up as she approached her rooms, she said as she stepped onto the first step, "Thank you. For walking me home, I mean." Her face burned brightly. He felt her shame beginning to worm itself into her every thought, every word. Would she ever feel right with herself again?

"Bea, I have to go out of town tomorrow, but I swear as soon as I get back, I'll come to you. We need to talk. I need to explain, about tonight." He felt desperate. He needed this chance to save them.

Bea lifted her head, pasted on one of her best casino smiles, and like a stranger accepting an invitation to a recital, said, "I look forward to your return." Then she disappeared into the house.

CHAPTER SEVEN

Preston practically jumped on Devlin and Walker as they departed the train, each carrying a small leather satchel. "They're gone. All of them this time," he accused harshly. "What the hell did you say to Bea, Devlin?"

Devlin, his heart racing at the words Preston was saying, lashed out. "Why blame me if you can't keep your woman under control? I don't own, Bea. She damn well does what she wants and she must have decided they had gotten what they could from this town." Shaking his head, he added, "But why leave again so soon? It's only been a few weeks and they all had jobs."

Preston tried to calm himself down. "I've been waiting for the two of you to return so I could get your help to figure out where they went. Then the train ran late and I couldn't contain my frustration and anger when you finally stepped off the car looking so carefree."

"When was the last time you saw them? Maybe we can get their trail and follow them right away, catch them before they settle-in and bring them back," Walker said turning to Preston for some answers.

Preston was concise. "I went to find Trudy when she didn't show up for work the day you two left town. The landlady told me the ladies had a death in the family out of town and they didn't know when or if they would be returning. That's it. I trailed them to the train station and again, dead end. I didn't know what time or what train or if they even took the train and it wasn't just to mislead me while they really left by stage. I went through their trash to see if there were any lists or notes about train schedules, but there was nothing."

Devlin, scrutinizing the busy station, said, "No, they left by train. I think the stage robbery left a sour taste in Bea's mouth if not Andy's. I bet the trail that you followed, Preston, was correct."

Walker did the same as if something there now would lead them to what happened three days ago, and it apparently did.

"Hey, you there. Were you working Tuesday morning?" Walker asked a porter stacking luggage on a wheeled cart. At the man's nod, Walker continued, "Did you see three very pretty young women traveling together?"

"Don't know, sir, there're a lot of people going through here a day," the young man answered.

"We," and Walker pointed to Devlin and himself, "took the five o'clock to the east. What other trains left around that time and were heading west or maybe north?"

The young man stared down at the worn floor, trying to picture that morning, recreate the scene and then shook his head saying, "Sorry, I don't remember three young women. I usually do." He smiled at the other men conspiringly. "There was a late comer for the six-fifteen, a widow and her two young daughters. I took their bags for them, but I don't recollect which train cart I put them on. It starts getting busy about then. Mostly business men or couples, you know, with families."

"I'll check with the ticket seller. See if he remembers a widow and two daughters," Devlin said and hurried in that direction.

The porter went back to his job and Walker was left to think about their missing women.

Approaching the ticket clerk, an older man, Devlin

placed a silver coin on the shelf in front of him, saying, "I'm looking for a woman."

Glancing at the coin but not any higher the ticket agent said, "I don't do that sort of thing but any of the drivers out front can take you to a place."

Devlin said firmly, "I'm looking for a woman in connection with a case."

That made the man behind the wrought iron gate glance up from his work and notice the marshal's badge plainly in sight on Devlin's wide chest. "Oh, sorry marshal, what kind of woman and when. I have a pretty good memory for faces," he said as he pushed the coin back towards Devlin.

"She would have been leaving on Tuesday morning early, but after the five o'clock east. Might have been buying three tickets," Devlin told the man but not saying anything about a widow.

"Tuesday morning? Let me check my records. I need to keep track of tickets sold, of course, hmmm. Oh, yes, now I remember, a widow bought tickets to Coyote Gulch. I took some note of it because, although, I couldn't see her face through the dark veil, she walked like a beautiful woman, you know, a sort of regal bearing and tall…she just floated across the platform."

The clerk seemed to be thinking back. "Had two other young women with her, real pretty they were. Two blonds, well one kind of a strawberry blond. Didn't have a lot of luggage. I figured they were travelling to a funeral. After all, as you probably know, Coyote Gulch isn't a place polite young ladies go if they don't have to," the older man said.

"Well, I thank you and you were right, you have a good memory. When's the next train to Coyote Gulch?"

Devlin finished, "I'll take three."

Devlin returned to a dissolute Walker and Preston and announced, "I got'em. They left right after we did. Probably would have run into them if the train had been late. They're posing as a widow and her two daughters, going to Coyote Gulch. I've got the tickets for us and it leaves in a little over three hours."

"Coyote Gulch? The ticket seller sure? I mean they wouldn't have a casino there, not the kind Trudy or Bea would work at. Would they?" Preston seemed unsure of what the women would do. "I know Trudy held back this information. I knew something had been different that last night I saw her, but I thought it was due to my passionate reaction to her or the fact I was pushing for marriage. Maybe if I hadn't forced her into agreeing to speak with her sisters about getting married, she'd still be with me."

Evidently able to understand Preston's concern, Devlin said, "Don't beat yourself up, Preston. We all put pressure on them one way or another. I think this all has to do with their reasons for moving from town to town all the time. Either someone is chasing them and they move on when they think he's found them or they move so they never have to worry that he'll find them."

"It's a man, you think? They're running from a man? Ex-husband or abusive husband? Not Trudy, I'd swear she's never been with a man." At the stares from the other men, Preston defended, "She's not cold to me, just that I can tell she's not experienced."

Walker said, "Calm down, I know what you mean. Andy's never been with a man before either, but I thought she was here waiting for me. Maybe I was wrong."

Devlin didn't say anything, which in itself was telling.

Walker continued, "I would have sworn she wouldn't lie to me, but she did. Not only that, but I think she was getting information from me to make sure we didn't run into each other at this station. I guess I'm a fool to think I meant more to her than I did."

Devlin broke into the commiseration party saying roughly, "Doesn't matter. They're acting suspiciously and we need to find out why. Preston, before we leave can you get some of the other offices involved in digging up everything you can about the sisters before Taxco. That's as far back as I went, but they came from out of state. I'll pay, but I would rather not have a contract."

"Not a problem. I'll say it's for an on-going investigation and they'll bill me here. That's where all the information will come, too, unless I have one of the agents forward it to me," Preston informed them.

The three men separated to make arrangements to be away for another few days only on personal business. If anyone were to realize they were all going off together it would have raised suspicions, but the two superiors didn't converse with one another. Walker always took a break when his marshal did as they usually worked as a team.

Arriving back at the station ten minutes before the train's departure they looked like different men. Each had a clean-shaven face, and clothing more fit for the desert town they were going to than the city. Devlin and Walker wore sheepskin coats over shirts and vests, tan trousers and boots with ten-gallon hats. Preston wore a two-tone gray wool hounds-tooth suit, covered with a long duster, short boots and black Homburg. All three carried a satchel and rifle as well as their hip weapons. Both Walker and Preston had boot knives they were well trained in using.

The long trip to Coyote Gulch was spent napping and thinking. Each man lost in thoughts of what they could have done or not done to prevent this trip being necessary. Devlin knew each man thought about what they would do with their respective woman when she was finally found. He knew each man was willing to forgive any sin or transgression as long as their woman returned to them. Devlin knew he did already. He also hoped Bea would be able to explain why she ran so he could help her. So, she would never feel the need to lie to him and hide what she and her sisters were up to.

Devlin had the most to think about, or at least, felt the guiltiest. If he hadn't made love to her, then Red wouldn't have run, he was sure of it. Other than pushing him away, making him keep his distance while she worked, there hadn't been any signs she wanted him gone.

Of course, there wasn't any signs she thought she was being followed either. What had Maurice said? Bea acted like a woman being followed by a man or searching for one? That had been his feeling, too. So, if Bea isn't being followed by a man then she was following one.

"Anyone got a map? Of Texas, at least?" As each shook their heads, Devlin said, "Next stop and I'll try to buy one."

"What if the girls got off the train between Lemmoxville and Coyote Gulch? I mean no one is held prisoner on a train. The tickets could have been a decoy." Walker worried aloud.

Devlin shook his head saying, "Bea is too frugal.

She wouldn't waste money on buying tickets to an out of the way town like Coyote Gulch and not need to go there. And she thinks the widow disguise would keep us from finding her, her red hair being the most conspicuous of the three. She thinks she's home free. We're going to have the element of surprise on our side."

"I hope so. Those three sisters have no idea how rough a town they're going to. And too close to the border for me to like the company they'll have in the hotels there. I'm worried they're already in trouble," Preston said, finally putting his fears out there in front of the other two men.

"We can't dwell on those things, Preston. Bea, I know, always carries a gun on her person. I take it she knows how to use it," Devlin said firmly.

Walker added, "Andy does, too. She had a derringer in the desert, but we didn't need to use it."

"That probably means Trudy does, also. That's three guns and at least three bullets. I guess that might cause a man to think twice," Preston said seemingly feeling a little more optimistic about the sisters' safety.

CHAPTER EIGHT

The train made a quick stop at Coyote Gulch, one of the southernmost towns being serviced by the railroad and town was stretching the meaning. The station was small and consisted of the ticket seller's office and a box room.

Grabbing their saddles from the freight car, the three men moved toward the building with the hotel sign over its porch. A plank façade made the building appear to have a third floor while most of the other buildings had a façade covering the fact, they lacked a second floor. All were in need of paint and a good cleaning. Some missing windows filled in with any piece of wood that was handy.

Hoisting their saddles to their shoulders, they began the walk on the dusty street between the buildings that must pass as the main boulevard. A couple of sleepy horses were in front of the saloon, but it was pretty quiet there, too. Although a lace curtain twitched in the window of the mercantile and Devlin thought he saw the silhouette of a man wearing a hat through the office marked 'doctor', no one showed their face.

Devlin studied the hotel's front room with its small sitting area. The sofa and two chairs with a couple of side tables and lamps near the lace covered front windows were unexceptional. Over all it was clean but faded by the hot Texas sun. The worn wooden front desk matched the wood on the stairs to the second floor and presumably the guestrooms. The owner's quarters were located through the doorway behind the desk, the odor of cooking wafting from behind it.

The owner of the hotel came up to the front desk as

soon as the men walked through the door. "May I help you, gentlemen? Come to mine for gold, have you?" His voice petered out as he saw the two badges showing plainly on the coats. "Looking for someone, Marshal? Maybe I can be of help," he offered readily, maybe too readily.

"Just need a couple of rooms, if you have 'em," Devlin said speaking for all three.

"Sure do, Marshal, and I can recommend the diner next door for your meals. Not very expensive and the portions are plentiful," he said while the three men noted he didn't talk up the taste.

When the hotel owner turned the check-in book around to face Devlin, he noted the name of Beatrice Jennings plus two and his heart skipped a beat. "I see we're not alone here. Anyone interesting?"

"Just a couple of young ladies. Not my usual clientele, but then they have to stay somewhere, don't they? Real polite and won't be back for a day or two so if you're worried about any noise or anything…that won't be a problem."

Devlin didn't comment but merely grunted. He knew he was going to get more information if he seemed unconcerned about his prey.

"That livery open?" Devlin asked. "Does it rent horses?"

"If he has any. Many are rented to take men up to the mining area, but they're sent back here once the men get settled or disheartened. Most men usually come back and leave, back east. Mining isn't just picking up nuggets from the ground, and many of these fellas have no idea about hard work under less than pleasant conditions. I get 'em as they come and as they leave."

The hotel owner told them, evidently deciding they weren't going to do any harm to his business or patrons, "There's a town closer to the big veins, but you need to have a horse to get there. The train don't go into those hills. If we had us a claims office, then this town would really pop off the map."

Another grunt from Devlin indicated that Walker should turn and go back out to the street to check out the livery.

Once outside, the men compared impressions of the hotel owner's information. "I saw Bea's signature in that ledger, using another last name, of course. Jennings, now." Devlin let the others know they were on the right trail although he figured they knew that. After all, three women traveling alone isn't very usual.

"I say we question the livery fella to see if the girls rented horses, too. If they're not in town then they probably rode out to the mining area," Preston surmised.

"Do you think they finally found the man they've been searching for? It seems kind of out of the way and not very busy for a town near a mining area," Walker said, staring around the almost empty street.

"Well, if they're at the site, and their bags are still here, then we'll run into them if we go toward the mining area, too. Like the man says, both coming and leaving. This is the only way out for them," Devlin said as they reached the livery.

Preston asked, unsure of what Devlin meant, "Are you suggesting that we wait here until they return?"

"Hell, no! They have no more sense than a fawn. They go anywhere thinking the three of them can protect one another and we all know that isn't true. I mean, any group of men out there without their women, any woman, could be driven to abuse one let alone three beautiful ladies," Devlin told him frustrated.

"Good, I was about to tell you we were going our separate ways. Now that I know where they went, I feel they are in even more danger and we need to get to them," Preston told the other two men.

"Look, let's get some horses and maybe some information, then start to the mining area yet tonight," Devlin told the other two, who nodded their heads in agreement.

Once in the livery it took a moment to find the thin, reedy man in the back of the building, sitting on a cot. "Ken I hep ya?" The voice sounded like one from a much older man, but the pile of cigarette stubs to his side might explain that.

"We need to rent three of your best horses and some directions to the mining fields," Devlin said, again taking point.

"We-e-ll, you boys are a little tall fer some of my mares so let's see if ya like the geldings I got." He slid open the rear barn style door to show off several horses moving nervously around the paddock.

"I like the looks of that gray, and the two solid brown ones with the black manes. Did I do well?" Devlin asked the livery owner.

"Got a good eye and I'm not just saying so. Those three were the top ones I had in mind fer ya, but the gray is a little feisty so don't put the city slicker on him." He laughed when Preston bristled at being called a city slicker.

"You rent any horses to three ladies in the last few days?" Walker asked.

"Naw, they asked but the price must have been too

steep. They go there anyways?" the owner asked. "Not an easy trek on foot."

"Let's get them saddled up. Walker, go over to that mercantile and get some food for the trail and anything else we may need. Preston and I can get things done here," Devlin said as the livery owner began the ritual of getting the horses inside and saddled that didn't want to do so.

Less than half an hour later, all three were settled in their saddles, their bags left in the rented room less the items they would need on the trail. Devlin and Preston both knew the way to the trails leading to the mining fields thanks to the talkative livery hand. The three men took off in a swirl of dust.

Riding at a very fast pace, first, because the horses were fresh and they would have to stop once the sun went down and second, and probably most important, because all three men were letting their fears take hold of them.

Just as it was turning dark, they spotted a trail fire up ahead. Evidently, they had come upon a group of miners heading to the field, too. Possibly they could share the camp and get more information about the fields from them.

Devlin was the first to swear. "Damn, it's them. We've found them already."

He sped up a little but pulled his horse to a stop, not wanting to ride right into the middle of the camp so remained on the trail. Jumping off the horse, he kept the reins and smiled at the tall redhead, her hair tucked up inelegantly into a bonnet.

The expression on her face was as if she saw a ghost, her hand going to her mouth, her gaze darting around searching for a place to flee. Before she could, the other two men rode up with wide smiles on their faces and each dismounted moving toward their respective woman.

At least the women were dressed for the cooler weather. Their skirts or dresses made of wool showed from under heavy coats and capes. All wore the more shielding poke style hat to protect them from the sun during the day and the cold at night. Knitted wool mittens and gloves covered their hands since the night air got crisp. Over-all, they didn't appear to be in need.

Expelling a deep breath, he waited for the explosion he felt was coming.

Bea was amazed at how the more casual western styled clothes made Devlin appear taller, wider and more masculine. She was used to his wearing boots and hat, but this was so much more. The wide belt buckle, the tighter trousers that fit against his thighs and his throat showing at the open shirt collar. Her mouth went dry as she tried to keep herself from staring.

Walker had gone directly to Andy, holding her to his body as he kissed her warmly on the mouth. Preston did much the same thing with Trudy. Both women happy to be held close to their man and neither trying to change positions in any way. Bea felt a tinge of envy at her sisters' good fortune. They, at least, found men who wanted a true relationship with them. More than a few nights in a warm bed.

There was a motion in the dark where the fire's light didn't shine and all three men went for their guns.

"Stop," yelled Bea and placed her hand on Devlin's hand. "It's just, Paco. He's been our guide to the fields. There's a pack mule, too."

Paco, a short gray-haired Mexican wearing baggy white shirt and pants tied at the waist and a wide brimmed sombrero hanging down his back stepped into the light, nodding his head with a tight smile on his face.

Walker was the first to let go of his gun. "Sorry, we thought the young ladies were alone. One of the reasons we're so glad to find them in one piece. Thanks for taking such good care of them."

Again, Paco nodded and set a pot near the fire where he was evidently going to start making a meal.

Each of the couples began talking quietly. Bea faced Devlin saying, "We did nothing wrong. You can't stop us and you can't keep following us like this."

"I'm not following them." And he moved his head to indicate the twins. "I'm following you. I told you we would need to talk when I got back to Lemmoxville and then I get back to find you gone—again."

"I don't owe you an explanation. I've given you more than enough," she said petulantly as she turned to pick up a couple of pieces of dead wood.

"That's one of the things we have to discuss," he said trying to get Bea to stop and face him.

Instead she gazed up into his eyes, a silent plea for him not to push her into this conversation, at least not now and not here.

"I understand. I'll wait till we get back to Coyote Gulch, but I'm not waiting past then," Devlin warned her. Bea nodded in acknowledgement but wasn't happy about it.

She watched as Walker handed over some canned food to Paco and they were added to the pot that soon smelled quite good. All felt pangs of hunger they had been ignoring the last few hours.

When they finally had pans of food in front of them, Paco took his to sit nearer his mule.

Devlin said, "All right ladies, we need to know what this trip was all about. I won't believe you were interested in mining anything so speak-up. Any one of you. We're listening." He took a spoonful of the savory stew trying to act as if this wasn't the most important conversation, he'd ever participated in.

Both of the twins looked at their older sister for direction and she finally took a deep breath, not touching her food. "I've been searching for someone who is very important to me. The twins have promised to help me, so we move every time I hear he may be somewhere. We are probably the closest to finding him here than we have ever been." Tears filled her eyes making her drop her head to her bent knees.

The twins gazed sadly at their older sister and the men all seemed to feel lousy for causing her to cry, even Devlin.

"How can we help, Red. Give us some information and let us do what we do best," Devlin said unable to take the guilt of her tears any longer.

Bea shook her head, but was crying too hard to speak, the twins started to get up to go to her. Instead, Devlin set his plate down and went to sit next to Bea, placing his arm around her.

"Look, Red, I know you don't trust me, but I swear I'll find this guy for you if that's what you want. These other two will help me, no charge, I swear it." Devlin's hand rubbed her back as she tried to stop crying.

She wiped her eyes with her skirt. "I've been trying to find him for so long. I've gotten so close and then he simply disappears again."

"I know the feeling," said Devlin dryly. "But if you'll stay in one place, hopefully in Texas, we men will find the man. Tell us everything you can about him."

There was a hesitation and then she began speaking. "His name is Elliot O'Malley, but he often goes by Mick. He's twenty-six and five-foot-eleven, slim but not skinny, or he wasn't the last time I saw him. Auburn hair and blue, blue eyes. Usually spends a lot of time indoors, in casino and gambling joints. Dresses snappy, bowlers and bright ties or vests most of the time."

As the tears sprang to her eyes, she said sadly, "I'm afraid he might be dead. The men on his claim said they bought it from him and he left, but he hasn't had the claim very long. He wouldn't have simply quit like that. I know it deep down." Then almost afraid to say it out loud, whispered, "I think the men killed him for the claim. They said they had a signed agreement but wouldn't show it to us."

The men passed a look among themselves and Walker asked, "Do you think they were lying to you, Bea?"

"I don't know. I mean I'm usually good at knowing when a man is telling the truth or not, but lately it doesn't seem to be dependable. I'm not sure, what did you think, Trudy?" Bea asked.

Trudy shook her head. "It seemed to me they were acting nervous. You know, wanted us out of there quickly and just seemed rushed or something. Uneasy."

"I got that feeling, too. They kept looking at one another and I thought it best we left as soon as we could," Andy told the group.

"Well, then, tomorrow we could go up there and have a talk with them. These badges often have men saying things they never thought of saying, nervous babbling," Walker said offering the help Devlin spoke of.

Paco collected the dirty dishes and utensils and went to clean them with sand.

Andy stood up while Walker spread a bedroll for them to lie on side by side. After all, they had spent other nights under the stars and were used to sleeping curled up together.

Preston and Trudy were copying them, talking quietly, and making a nest for the night.

Glancing at her sisters disgustedly, Bea took her blanket a little way from the fire. She wouldn't tell her sisters not to lay beside the men but refusing to do so herself. Everyone was quiet. Bea content with her choice to sleep alone, but near the others when Devlin came up behind her.

Bea hissed pulling the blanket up to her nose. "Go away. I don't want to have you near me, again."

"It's going to get colder tonight, Red, and even sleeping in your coat won't keep you warm enough. Come on, don't cut off your nose to spite your face. Let me sleep snuggled up with you. Remember it's going to keep me warm, too. Everyone else has a warm body up against them. Even Paco has the mule," he pointed out.

"Just stop talking and don't touch me. You know what I mean." Bea gritted her teeth so that he wouldn't hear them chatter.

Taking off his coat, he placed the heavy sheepskin open over them both as he laid down behind her, curving toward her and pulling her into his body. Bea tried to stay laying straight, forcing her body into rigid denial, but she felt the cold faster and soon curled into the fetal position, allowing Devlin to curve protectively around her.

"Now that no one can hear us, tell me why you ran

without letting me talk to you," he whispered in her ear, his breath making chills run down her spine with each word.

"It doesn't matter. It was a mistake and I'm sorry I let myself down," Bea told him honestly.

"What does that mean? Making love with me was a letdown?" There was a pause as if he didn't know what to say. "I'm sorry. I should have asked more questions before I took you to bed. I might have been able to make it easier on you," he sounded contrite.

"It's not that. It's that you think I'm…I'm of easy virtue. That I sleep with men…that I'm wicked and of lowest morals." Crying quietly, she kept letting the descriptive words paint her in worse and worse terms.

"I never said any such things. Why would you think I thought those things about you? I was fascinated by you and I acted on that as I thought you had, too. You're gorgeous and any man would feel himself lucky to attract you."

At her silence, Devlin added, "I was experienced at your age. Why would I expect you not to be? And then there's the man you're hunting for. I knew there was someone you were hiding from me. Someone you were close to at one time. I don't think less of a woman for having loved someone. Being a virgin doesn't make you an angel and not being one doesn't make you a whore."

Devlin murmured, quietly for her ears only, "Red, do you understand what I'm trying to say? I'm not holding you up to any higher standards because you're a female."

That did make Bea less upset. Knowing he didn't think badly of her for going to his room and that he hadn't guessed her secret after all. That she cared for

Devlin more than she should have allowed herself to. She settled down to sleep, finally able to relax for the first time in days.

During the night, Devlin kissed Bea on the back of her neck and the side of her face turned toward him. His hand cupped a breast while his thumb toyed with the nipple that was beginning to become interested in his attention. He moaned and ground his hips into her fanny, as if trying to find some sort of relief for his arousal. Rucking Bea's skirt up little by little until his hand could reach her inner core, he stroked his fingers into the satiny warmth, finding the hidden nub waiting there.

"Red, let me show you how we could be together, you and me. Let me make love to you. I'm having a hell of a time trying to sleep knowing you're there so close," Devlin said into her neck.

Bea arched into his hand, urging him on to more intimate contact, remembering how good he had made her feel. How only he could make her feel.

Devlin must have unbuttoned his trousers because his erection was strategically placed when he penetrated her slowly, his fingers toying with the nubbin as he entered and receded again and again, in long slow strokes. She felt the beginning of her climax and he increased the pace to please her, even more as she began to become vocal.

"Shhhh, Red, not this time. We don't want to let the others hear us," he whispered and she bit down on her lower lip letting the spasms convulse through her body as Devlin stiffened in his release deep inside of her.

Devlin didn't move, wanting to retain the contact with her. But his thoughts were all over the place. He hadn't meant to do this when he offered to sleep next to her to keep her warm. He hadn't meant to take her from the back without the normal readying. He hadn't meant to have sex with her again at all let alone without protection. What kind of a fool was he becoming not to follow his own rules when it came to this woman? His plan had been to take things slowly when he found her again. Give her time to decide where she thought they would be six months from now. He was too drawn to her hoping she wanted to be with him, as well. How was he to convince her of what he wanted when he wasn't sure himself? And how was he to explain it to her in the morning?

In the morning, it was too late.

CHAPTER NINE

He watched as Bea left their bed at first light beginning to help Paco get the fire going and the breakfast started. Her sisters and their bedmates began to move, also, since they couldn't waste daylight on these shorter days. He wasn't sure how to go about finding their new relationship. He knew Bea wouldn't want her sisters to know and definitely not the other men.

This wasn't an area he was comfortable navigating. He had never kept a woman although there had been some he revisited if he was in their area. He never had one he wanted to return to repeatedly no matter where his work took him. Perhaps he could think about settling down, ask to be stationed in one area more than another. Would that be possible? He'd have to think on it. Right now, he had fences to mend and promised himself by the time they reached town and the train, Red would be his.

Devlin finally came up to the camp's fire saying, "Walker, we need to see to the horses so we can get back to Coyote Gulch and still make the train."

Bea turned toward Devlin. "I thought you were going to search for Mick? Didn't you mean it?" All eyes were on him including Paco's.

Devlin looked at Bea but couldn't ask the question he wanted an answer to. *What was last night about if you still want to find this man?* But aloud he said, "I…I guess I thought you had changed your mind. But, ah, I can ride up and check out the men on the claim. Walker, you want to go with me?"

"I'll stay with the ladies then, Devlin. They've been walking because they didn't have enough money to rent horses as well as the guide and still have train fare home," Preston explained. "I'll escort them as protection and you can find us along the trail on your way back if we don't reach town before you return."

After a quick breakfast, Bea watched Devlin and Walker head towards the claim sites with directions from Paco. The rest continued towards the town and their rooms at the hotel. Preston walked, leading the horse with one then another of the women riding. He refused to take a turn, explaining he wouldn't ride while women walked. Trudy walked beside him, talking and sometimes laughing. Both enjoying themselves despite the cold and the rough terrain.

The larger group stopped for the night. Paco again setting up the campsite and making a very edible meal and again cleaning up after it. Everyone else gathered wood for the nighttime fire before it became too dark. Preston figured they would be in town the next evening if nothing unusual happened on the trail.

They were about to bed down for the night, Trudy next to Preston which made Bea uneasy since she now knew how easy it was to sin under the guise of keeping warm. She wanted to warn her younger sister, but then watched Preston with Trudy and Bea realized they were past the warning stage. They were already in love.

The sound of the horses coming from behind them had Preston telling the women to get well back into the shadows while he made sure his rifle was in his arms as welcome to any strangers. Then the gray with Devlin riding him and Walker came into the fire's glow and the rest relaxed. All except Bea that was, worried her fears would be confirmed, that Mick had been killed.

The men got off their horses and Paco came for them, telling the men he would take care of the tired animals. That they should eat as soon as he made more supper.

"Don't bother, Paco. I'll open a couple of cans and we'll eat them cold. Won't be the first time and I'm too hungry to wait for anything to be heated anyway," Walker told the old Mexican.

Bea came forward toward Devlin with fear and hope fighting to take control of her emotions. "Did you find out anything new? Is Mick dead?"

Gazing at her, he put her out of her misery. "I don't think so. At least, those men on his claim didn't kill him. We talked a little but I finally got them to tell me about you. They were afraid you were his wife and had some kind of claim to their site. They didn't want to say the wrong thing so tried to say nothing about the sale."

Placing her hand out to keep from collapsing, Bea folded down to her knees saying, softly, "I was sure they had killed him. I almost talked myself into being strong enough to hear the words but these words are so much better. If he's still alive, I still have a chance to find him."

The sleeping arrangements were different than the night before. Bea and Andy were already in a bed together so Devlin and Walker slept separately. He knew neither were as happy with their situation as they had been the night before.

In the morning after a quick breakfast, Bea paid Paco the rest of what she owed him and the little man went off in a different direction from both the mining fields or the town. The other six, a woman in front of each man, rode on toward the town, trying to make time while not wearing out the horses.

Bea didn't talk with Devlin. She was too preoccupied with where to go from here. Watching her sisters with the men in their lives made her realize how selfish she had become to think they should dedicate their lives to finding Mick simply because she had. Bea didn't want to admit it, but her sisters were grown women and they evidently had found the men they wanted to spend the rest of their lives with.

She would have a family meeting again and would set the twins free. Free to marry if that's what they wanted or stay together in the city while Bea continued with her quest to find Mick.

Finally, the tired desert town came into sight no cleaner or more populated than when they left it just a few days before. The horses sped up to a trot when they smelled their home stalls, but the men wanted to drop their ladies at the hotel so reined their horses to a stop there first.

As Andy was being let down unto the boardwalk in front of the hotel, she glanced up the street to see a man mount his horse, a brown horse with a white star on its face and white on its two front feet.

Andy froze then said, her voice wavering, "Walker, Walker, that man's the one who shot the horse."

Walker spun and urged his horse after the one that was now under full gallop when the rider evidently saw the badge on the coat of the man showing interest in him. Devlin followed Walker, not really understanding who they were chasing. But knowing his deputy, didn't hesitate to send his horse after the other two.

Going to Andy who was shaking at this point, Bea hurried both twins into the hotel and their room. The women ordered hot water and went about cleaning up, washing their hair and getting ready to take the train back to a more civilized area, trying not to worry about Devlin and Walker chasing a desperate killer into the desert. Preston acted as guard, watching for any possible danger to the three women, but the town seemed pretty calm now.

Devlin and Walker came back to the hotel after leaving the horses at the livery. The man from the robbery had gotten away. His horse was fresh and he knew the terrain and all the nooks and crannies available to hide in. The rental horses had been tired from carrying two people all day and couldn't keep up. The lawmen had walked them back to town.

Over an early dinner that night, Walker told everyone at the table what he was able to find out about the man he chased into the desert. "He's been staying over the saloon using the name of Clive Winters. Met up with some other fellows a couple of weeks ago, and then they rode out without him. He told the bartender he wouldn't be back for a while. No specific date of return."

Devlin added, "He didn't take extra provisions with him so he must plan on meeting up with someone. There's not a lot of places for him to get food and water this time of year. I bet they're not far, less than a day or two, but no way of telling in what direction."

"I was going to break into his room before it was cleaned-up but I couldn't get upstairs when we questioned the bartender. There are back stairs and I'll check those out when it gets dark," Walker reported.

"I want to come, too," said Andy. "I can get you into the room without you having to break the door down."

Walker was already shaking his head when Bea said, "You can use my tools. They're more complete than yours."

The three men stopped eating, some with their forks

half-way to their mouths.

"What do you mean?" asked Preston, suspicious of the two women.

Trudy stared down at the napkin in her lap and the other two sisters glanced guiltily at each other.

"Just something our father taught us, in case we lost our keys," Andy said with a smile that wouldn't melt butter.

None of the men believed her but put the information away for another time. Devlin would let Walker get the information out of Andy. He knew getting information out of Bea would be impossible, at least for a while. He must be back in her bad books again, although, he admitted, there was reason. He never should have made love to her again. What was it about this woman? He went weeks, sometimes months without any sexual release and now he couldn't go a couple of days without fantasizing about everything he would like to do with her.

It humbled him to think she had that much power over him. But he had to admit that she did. Once that was out in the open, he would be able to focus on his job again and compartmentalize Bea to after-hour enjoyment, someone to meet and make love to when his other duties were fulfilled.

But first he would have to convince her she wanted, no needed him, as well. That this Mick was running from her, possibly even hiding from her so she should turn her regard somewhere else. This other must have been a young love and she took it more seriously than the man had. Bea seemed to think she still had a chance with him.

Devlin wanted to argue. Wanted to tell her she had no need to find this man. That Devlin would take care of her, keep her safe, make sure she needed nothing. But that didn't seem to be what Bea wanted. He always came up short when it came to what Bea wanted.

After dinner, everyone but Walker went back to the hotel for an early night. They wanted to be ready for the first train through in the morning. Devlin stayed outside to smoke one of his few cigarettes of the day. Bea and Andy went upstairs. He never suspected Andy would continue right back outside, down the rear stairs, and behind the buildings to the saloon. Preston and Trudy sat in the parlor area for a few moments alone.

Walker was at the top of the outside stairs of the saloon, having checked to see who and how many patrons were inside and their state of inebriation. To see if any of them were sober enough to notice him breaking into a room. He felt rather than heard someone on the steps below him and turned, his hand on his still holstered gun.

"Andy, what the hell? I could have shot you," he said in a harsh whisper.

She whispered in return, "No you wouldn't have, you know what you're shooting at before you do so. I brought the tools. It will be faster my way." She went through the door before him. "What's the room number? And don't tell me you didn't get it from the bartender. I know you too well."

She quietly walked along the edge of the hall where the boards were less likely to squeak. There was some noise from downstairs to cover the couple's footsteps, boot scuffing the wood floorboards, men talking and a woman's fake laughter.

"Six," said Walker disgustedly, not sure if it was with Andy or himself for being such a pushover.

Andy tried the door, but it was kept locked, probably to keep any non-paying customers from sleeping off a drunk for free. Kneeling by the door, Andy inserted a piece of metal and then another into the lock wiggling them before turning the knob as it opened. Both of them slid through the door and shut it behind them.

The room didn't have too many places to search. A bed with thin mattress, a wood spindle-backed chair, a washstand and a side table with lamp. Walker lit the lamp but kept the wick turned low.

Andy went to check out the trashcan. "I'm praying the man doesn't chew. Nothing is more disgusting than to find your hand up to the wrist in spit, and to my great chagrin, I know what that feels like."

It must be her lucky day because she found a couple of pieces of paper, which she took out and smoothed on the rough table.

"Okay, I can make out that it's a list, just says food at the top and then rope, burlap bags, grain and, oh, oh, dynamite," Andy read out loud. "What would this man want with dynamite?"

Walker replied without much thought, "Train robbery, blow the tracks to stop the train, mine robbery, drop sticks of powder down the shaft to cause a distraction, throw sticks near cattle to cause a stampede and then rustle the scattered herd…."

"I get it, a lot of criminal stuff so that doesn't leave us with any one trail to follow. He could have gone anywhere to do anything," Andy said grouchily.

"We don't have any trail to be following. I only took you with me last time because I didn't have a choice but we are not partners in getting these men. Devlin and I will track them down," Walker told her firmly. "What's that other stuff you found?"

"Cigarette paper and a punched ticket stub from the train. He's been to Lemmoxville, within the last week. We could have been on the same train for goodness sake it's so close in date," Andy said. "What a small world this is sometimes."

"Now that is of an interest to me," said Walker. "Let's get out of here but we'll take these two pieces of evidence with us. Maybe Devlin will have a better idea of this guy's plans."

Devlin was waiting outside the saloon, not far from the privy and wasn't happy to see Andy at all. "What don't you understand, young lady, about staying out of an ongoing investigation? We tell you more than we should as it is. I don't want to have to explain to my superiors how I got a girl shot or taken hostage while hunting down an outlaw. Walker, you know better than this."

Andy defended Walker immediately. "It wasn't his fault. I came up to him after he had already started to find the room. We did find something interesting, but nothing that told us where he was going or who he was meeting."

Then seeing the hard look Devlin gave Walker, she must have thought it best if she made herself scarce and walked quickly towards the rear stairs of the hotel.

Once Andy was out of hearing, Walker asked redundantly, "Why do you suppose these girls know how to pick locks?"

Devlin answered anyway, "Don't know, but maybe that's why they interest us."

CHAPTER TEN

The morning train was on time and it didn't stay long at the station. Devlin and Bea's groups the only travelers and no cargo being taken on or off. Preston sat next to Trudy, their heads together already in their quiet conversation. Walker took the window seat and Andy sat beside him, his hand finding hers as soon as she was settled.

That left Bea and Devlin. Bea sat down and hoped that Devlin, with his large, male body would sit in a seat by himself. After all, there were plenty of empty seats in the passenger car. But just to be his disobliging self, he sat down next to Bea forcing her to scoot closer to the outside wall, which felt cold, even through her cape.

Devlin must have known because he placed his arm behind her and pulled her closer to his side, while Bea tried to sit stiffly next to him.

"Relax, Red, nothing can happen in front of the others." And he left his hand holding on to her around her ribs where she could feel his thumb rub the side of her breast as if of its own accord.

"Stop that," she hissed. "It's inappropriate."

"What? Oh, sorry, I guess I like the feel of that material, kind of like satin, isn't it?" Devlin said honestly. "I was unaware of my thumb's movements…but not of my hand's placement."

Staring out the window at the same landscape she had been walking through for the last five days, Bea let out an exasperated sigh. She was hoping this train trip would seem to go faster than the one she arrived on. She had been so sure they had caught up to Mick. That he would be there, that they could be together now that her father was dead. Mick and her father had never got along, but that was no longer an issue. She had to find him. She couldn't think of Mick without missing him these days.

Too many things in her life were changing and she didn't like feeling out of control, not having plans in place for the three of them. Now they were backtracking to Lemmoxville where the trail for Mick was dead and cold. Bea would need to have that family talk soon. Let the twins go their own ways while she continued on hers.

Devlin left Bea to her own thoughts while he concentrated on how to capture the elusive lady. How to convince her to forget about this Mick and allow him to take care of her. If he wasn't mistaken the twins were already spoken for and Preston wasn't a man to merely sleep with a woman. He had 'marriage' written all over him. And Walker was a lost cause. No need to even try to bother talking him out of taking Andy on. No, both those two men were lost causes.

He was thinking ahead to the next few weeks, too. He and Walker would get rooms again in the little hotel he was familiar with. The ladies would get their rooms, maybe at the same house as before or maybe they could find a little house of their own where the men could be welcomed. To hell with the neighbors and what they thought.

He'd offer help with the expenses since he knew this trip had cost Bea most of her savings. Devlin felt himself get angry just thinking of Bea having to go back to work at a casino, working nights letting men ogle her body, her beauty. No, he'd make her accept his money. She wasn't going to put herself out there in a dangerous position, again.

He wouldn't be around all the time to protect her.

He'd go on assignments and then come home to her. To her passion, to her body. It would all be his.

After the nearly two-day ride, the men's beards were fairly thick, while the women couldn't wait for baths and clean clothes. The soot that the train's engine spewed off, settled into everything and what once appeared white was now a dingy gray.

Bea refused to have the men accompany them while they searched for rooms to rent. And absolutely forbade the men from getting them rooms at the same hotel as Devlin and Walker stayed at. Bea never wanted to face that smirking desk clerk ever again.

Allowing the twins to stay with Preston who owned a small house not far from the commercial district, she gave direct orders to Preston to remember Trudy wasn't to be compromised in any manner. Preston seemed offended, but then acknowledged the command and escorted the ladies and their luggage to his home until Bea found proper accommodations for the three of them.

Bea went to the home she rented rooms at the first time they were in Lemmoxville, but that widowed lady had rented the rooms to a friend of about the same age. That meant buying a paper to see if there was something suitably inexpensive and in a safe neighborhood because she, at least, would be working a gaming table of some kind. It didn't matter exactly where now because she wouldn't be getting any new information on Mick.

The job would be used to build up her coffers once more before setting off to find Mick, possibly on her own for the first time in her life. But it didn't matter. She had made a promise and taking care of the twins was almost over, something to be passed on to their husbands. She would also be free for the first time to travel faster, fewer encumbrances to maneuver around.

Bea went to Preston's address that night tired and disheartened. Everyplace she went to that day had been disappointing, even the ones that seemed out of her budget. Families, now that harvesting was over, were flocking into the bigger towns to find winter work and taking up the less expensive housing. She would need to have the family talk sooner than she planned, take her leave of the twins although she hated to think of them on their own. Of course, they wouldn't be alone. She needed to remember they were old enough, at nineteen, to decide their own future and it seemed they both had found men, good men, to live the rest of their lives with. It was time, the right time, to separate.

Preston had made his intentions perfectly clear. Walker cared for Andy but was he the marrying kind or was he too like Devlin to change his ways? Bea hoped Andy knew and wasn't going to be hurt as Bea had been.

Preston's house was a single story with a small front yard fenced from the sidewalk and street. Walking up the narrow brick path to the front porch, Bea took the three steps up as the door opened and Trudy was there all smiles. Once inside, Bea saw a pleasantly decorated room with square-backed sofa and matching side chairs. Two marble turtle topped tables holding oil lamps, both with yellow painted glass bowls, sat on either side of the sofa with a third wooden topped table between the chairs. There were oil paintings of pastoral scenes and the coal heating stove had center place. A dining room could be seen that led to the kitchen at the back of the house. There were two bedrooms and a water closet off a hall to the side of the dining room.

The house smelled deliciously of roasted pork,

biscuits and something with cinnamon.

"We've bathed and feel so much better for it. Dinner can wait a while. There's a tub set up in the back room and plenty of hot water. Just yell out when you want one of us to rinse your hair for you," Trudy said, speaking as the woman of the house already, allowing Preston's hospitality to spread to her sisters as well.

"Thank you, that sounds lovely and the dinner smells wonderful as well so I'll hurry my bath. I need to be out of these clothes." She saw herself in a mirror then said, "No wonder no one had any rooms for us." She hurried towards the room behind the kitchen to the waiting tub.

In less than half an hour Bea reappeared to find Walker and Devlin in the parlor. Devlin's eyes lit up when he saw her but he didn't make a comment. Trudy called everyone to the table, which was crowded but no one cared after tasting the lovingly produced meal.

"Ladies, this is delicious," Walker said taking another mouthful of mashed potatoes and gravy.

"Yes, it really is, you are all excellent cooks," Preston added not to be out done by Walker.

"I had nothing to do with the meal, so all the compliments go to Trudy and Andy," confessed Bea.

"But you taught us how to cook, Bea, so in a way you're responsible for the dinner's outcome," Trudy said magnanimously to her older sister.

Bea smiled at Trudy for trying to share the compliments but Bea didn't care if the twins received praise when it was their due. Did the twins think Bea didn't want them to be successful? Everything seemed to come down to that much overdue family talk.

After the cinnamon spice cake and coffee, the ladies

cleared the table and cleaned up. The men spent some time in the parlor, but then left after saying it had been a long day. They made arrangements to reconvene back there in the morning.

What for, thought Bea. They weren't planning on searching for Mick with her, and she didn't give a rat's ass about the stage robber since he hadn't harmed Andy. Bea shook her head at her own bad temper. She really was too tired to think rationally tonight. She needed to sleep.

Preston had given up his room, which was a little larger and had a wider bed. The three sisters were used to sleeping together and soon were all tucked up.

Trudy said into the darkness, "Bea, I need to talk to you about something."

"Have you made love with Preston, yet?" Bea asked doggedly, too tired to be polite.

"No, never! Preston wants us to wait until we're married," Trudy said, seeming to take umbrage to Bea's callous question.

"Then it can wait till morning. I'm too tired to think straight. I love you both, good night," Bea said as she fell asleep.

"We love you, too, Bea," said Trudy to her practically snoring older sister.

In the morning after a light breakfast, Preston headed to his office to check in after his sabbatical and that left the three young women alone for once. Sitting in the parlor facing one another, Bea began.

"I want to thank you both for putting up with being dragged around the country. We started in Illinois and now find ourselves in Texas where we will probably go our separate ways."

With no denial from the twins, she continued, "I appreciated everything you've given up to help me find Mick, but I know he's more important to me than to you. After all, you hardly knew him. You were still in the schoolroom when he left me. I want you to feel free to go your own way, to say you want to stay here if that's your wish. You aren't obligated to me in any way, even as sisters."

Trudy, her eyes sad with the truth, explained, "Preston wants to marry me. Of course, he's wanted that for a while now and it isn't fair to him to keep moving away, promising to come back some day. I want to be with him, as a wife, but I don't want to lose you two in the process." Tears filled her eyes and ran down to drip off her quivering chin.

"It's natural for families, no, sisters, to go their own ways, even twins. Did you think we would always live together? Wouldn't that get a little cramped with all our husbands in one house, and then there would be the children," Bea said teasingly, but truthfully.

Andy added, "I know what you're feeling, Trudy, but I understand, too. Walker has been trying to get me to marry him. He says I can live anywhere I want within the state and he will make that town his headquarters. He gets assignments all over the area so where he lives isn't that important. He makes enough money to support a family and we love each other. There's no reason to wait unless I go with Bea to find Mick." The tears in her eyes were in sympathy with her twin.

Bea smiled saying lightly, trying not to let the tears show, "Well, that's settled then. My little sisters are going to beat me to the altar. That must make me a full-fledge spinster then, doesn't it? Have any dates been set?" She watched the twins as both of them stared at the carpet on the floor.

"Come on, I'm not disappointed in you. I'm really not. I'll be able to travel fastest on my own, react to news of Mick without worrying about housing and luggage and what all for three ladies. Please don't feel guilty because you have your men to love. I'll find my own one day." She pushed her younger sister's knees to get them to look up at her. "When are the weddings?"

"Preston would like it to be as soon as possible. He's, umm, regretting his promise to wait until we're married." Trudy smiled shyly at the implications of what she told her sisters.

Andy, ever the more practical twin, admitted, "We haven't talked of dates since I told him I had to stay and help Bea. I hate to think of you out there by yourself, Bea, but you have Devlin to call on for help. And I can see where Trudy and I could be an encumbrance when travelling and finding proper housing."

Bea softened her voice. "I didn't mean to call you encumbrances. Simply that one can travel faster alone. This is as it should be. You two should find the love and happiness I'm searching for. A family to make up for the one we never had as children."

Trudy and Andy said in unison, "It's agreed." Then laughed at each other as Trudy finished, "We'll get married and I'll live here with Preston."

"And Walker and I will get married and I hope to live here in town near Trudy," Andy said smiling at Bea. "Then you'll be able to always find us. I'll make sure you can find one or the other of us here whenever you need."

"I appreciate your help and I love you both," Bea told them with a smile knowing her heart held the truest possible love.

"And we both love you," Andy told her older sister.

Returning from his office, Preston said, "I've talked with Devlin and Walker. They sent a wire telling their superiors about the stagecoach robber they chased and they're waiting for orders as to whether they are to follow up or if there's a man closer to that area already." Looking around at the red-rimmed eyes he asked, "What happened?"

"Just a family talk. Congratulations, I hear you two are getting married," said Bea happily.

Preston turned to Trudy and opened his arms as she floated into them. "Really? You're going to marry me and stay here?" he asked seemingly afraid she was going to tell him it had been a joke.

"As soon as you want. I'm so happy. And Walker and Andy are going to be married, too. He said she could stay in town, that where he lived didn't affect his job," Trudy told him accepting his kiss.

Offering gallantly, Preston said, "Then, Bea, you can stay here with Trudy and me, as long as you don't mind us leaving you alone every once in a while."

"I refuse to play gooseberry but thank you for the offer. I'll make my own way. I found rooms today that would accommodate one woman, but not three so I may stay around for a while until I can build up my savings again," she told her future brother-in-law.

"If it's a matter of money, I can help you out. I've been a bachelor a long time and have built up a stake," he offered generously.

"No, you will need that as soon as the babies start coming. Besides, I take pride in my talent and there are always casinos and gaming halls that need good dealers," she said noting the red flush that came into his face when she spoke of babies. Trudy was right, this man was ready to have a wife.

Later that evening, Walker showed up to see Andy. She told him about the family meeting and the outcome. "I can't see why we should wait then, either, Honey. We can find a house probably or an apartment. It wouldn't take more than a day or two. Get married before I get the assignment in Coyote Gulch or somewhere else in the state."

Preston said, "I saw a house for rent sign, but they want a signed lease of six months. That's why I knew it wouldn't work out for the ladies. It's furnished because the woman passed away and her son lives right next door. He would probably be impressed that Walker is a lawman. We can talk with him tomorrow morning and then get in touch with the minister. The church I attend will certainly be happy to do both wedding services."

"Or we could have a double ceremony, it's not that uncommon for sisters to do so, especially twins," Trudy said bouncing with delight at the idea.

With hope in his eyes, Walker turned to Andy asking, "Would tomorrow be too soon for you? Do you need more time to be sure?"

"I've been sure, Walker. I just had to make sure you were," Andy said practically.

Bea looked at the happy couples feeling a tug at her heart but not for Mick, as usual. Instead, the tall lean frame of Devlin flashed into her mind. But she knew men better than most and he wasn't like these others. Marriage and making a family weren't in his plans even if he showed a preference to Bea at the moment. He was used to loving and leaving and Bea wanted just the opposite. Besides, Mick was still out there and she needed to find him. She felt she came close in Coyote Gulch and possibly with only herself to care for she would be able to catch up with him. Become the family she was driven to reclaim.

CHAPTER ELEVEN

By the time Devlin arrived at the house all hell seemed to be breaking lose. There were hatboxes and tissue paper and flowers covering every piece of furniture in Preston's once neat home. Walker and Preston came in from outside all grins, ignoring the mess around them and called for their respective twin.

"All set, Darling," Preston said as he took Trudy into his arms for a very welcoming kiss.

To Devlin's astonishment, Walker grabbed Andy and kissed her on the mouth, and then did so again. Devlin wasn't sure what was going on, but he was ready for his kiss from Bea when she came in and shot him down.

Bea said coldly, "Devlin, we weren't expecting you. Does Walker need to leave on assignment?"

"Haven't heard back, yet. Winter's trail will be dead cold by the time the powers that be get their plans together." He was disappointed at Bea's cool reception.

"Well, that's too bad, I'm sure, but none of my concern right now. The twins have decided they want a double-wedding ceremony, so while the men were out arranging their part, we women did ours. We went shopping. Now both brides have new hats, veils, gloves and shoes. A few personal items that the grooms can discover after the wedding…" Which comment brought wide grins to both grooms. "And flowers," Bea concluded.

"And a mess," said Devlin, not in the least happy with the outcome of the day after his plans to get Bea into private living quarters where he could visit her. Where they could make love without worrying about going home to another bed. He had been depending on that, but then when he thought about it this was even better.

She wouldn't need to worry about her sisters, any longer. What they thought about her being with Devlin, what anyone thought about them being together. After this quick re-calculation, Devlin became almost jovial with Walker and Preston, making those two men wary of his motives.

Walker and Devlin left with a little pressure from all the women since they said they had too much to do before the morning ceremony. The rental house had been procured and Bea told everyone she had a single room in the same rooming house they had stayed at before. Everything was taken care of when the women finally made it into bed.

Even with the excitement, the twins fell asleep relatively quickly, leaving Bea worrying as to whether she was doing the right thing. The men the twins had chosen were good, strong, and caring men. She held no worry for their welfare. The city was fairly safe and prosperous and both men had savings and prospects to continue being able to provide for their wives and families.

And there was the crutch of it…families. The twins will make their own families while Bea was still driven to find hers. To find Mick to make her feel complete again, the way she was when he was still part of her life, her love. Tears trickled down from Bea's closed lids as she cried for what may never be again, cried for her loss and for her inability to face the truth that Mick might be gone from her forever.

The three women and two men made it to the church

as a group. Both brides wore their best gowns. Andy's was a pale green to go with her hazel eyes while Trudy's was a pale peach bringing out the highlights in her blond hair. No one besides the minister and his wife who was to play the organ for the wedding ceremony and be the second witness along with Bea was present.

The minister was a pleasant older man who said this was his first wedding for twins. He began the traditional service then had both Walker and Preston placing rings on their respective wives' fingers and ending with both kissing their brides with restrained passion.

Afterwards, in front of the church, Bea excused herself which neither couple argued with. Bea told them she had sent her bags on to the rented room. Actually, she planned to begin her new life in a new town. One where she might be able to find a trail and information about Mick from the man who had lost the gold claim to Mick in the card game. It's all she had to live for now - finding Mick. Kissing each twin, she waved them off to their perspective homes as she waited to get a cab to take her to the train station.

Preston and Trudy arrived home first. Trudy shyly offered to make her new husband a meal.

He smiled shaking his head, saying, "I'm not hungry for food, Darling. I've been waiting weeks for us to be alone and all I want is you."

He removed his suit coat and vest, rolling up his shirtsleeves. Then added as Trudy walked to stand behind the chair, "Are you afraid of me?"

"Don't be silly, I'm not afraid of you," she said, but everything about her read as fear to the investigator.

"You're not afraid of me, but you are afraid of the marriage act, of making love. Do you know what it entails?" he asked calmly deciding he should sit down and not intimidate his small wife with his height.

"Bea explained it, and answered our questions last night," Trudy told him honestly.

"Did something she say to you make you afraid? Did she dissuade you from it in any way?" Preston asked still calmly, trying to find out if the unmarried older sister caused his bride to be skittish.

"Umm, she said that love making could be very pleasant, wonderful in fact between people who love one another." Then she hesitated, "But that it will hurt. The first time, there's no way around it and I'm not good with pain. I mean, I thought I would be. I love you ever so much, Preston, but now, now that it's time, I don't know if I can go through with it."

"Then it won't happen now. We'll wait until you're ready. I wanted to be married to you, to be able to protect you, to be by your side all day and all night. I have what I want, for now. When you feel the time is right, then you and I can explore the rest together."

He patted the sofa next to him. Trudy let out the breath she probably hadn't known she was holding and sat next to him.

Pulling her onto his lap, allowing her derriere to comfort his erection, he said, "I'm glad you were able to talk with me, Darling. I never want you to keep things from me and I'll always be open with you. Can we still kiss and may I still touch you like we used to do?"

"I've always loved kissing you, Preston. I can't imagine being with you and not having you kiss and touch me." Trudy pressed herself against his chest.

Preston was happy to oblige his new wife and put all his desire and passion into the kisses, letting his hand first roam over her back and then work its way to her breasts, sliding into the wide neckline of the gown so that he cupped the ample swell he found there. Trudy responded by pushing herself upwards, trying to keep her body in contact with his hand.

"Do you want more?" Preston asked, his breath coming faster than normal.

"Is there more then? I like this quite a lot," Trudy said inflaming Preston to consider all that he would like to be doing.

"Let me undo your gown in back. I'll show you what more there is," he said as he did as he told her.

Once the buttons were undone, the gown fell off her shoulders forming a puddle at her waist. He dispensed with the corset and camisole to expose her bare breast to his gaze and touch. Soon his hand was replaced by his mouth, which tongued the rigid peaks and suckled first one than the other. Trudy leaned back and offered herself up to him like a flower opening to the rain.

Preston let his hand go to the bottom of her skirts and stoked his hand up her stocking covered leg to the top where he found the soft, warm flesh. He kissed her as he made little circles with his thumb, getting more and more excited himself. Finally, unable to hold himself back, he touched her most intimate area, surprised when she moved her hips so that his hand slid between her legs, touching the curls covering her mound more intimately.

"Hmmm," Preston found himself moaning, wanting this and so much more, but knowing it may be a while before he could consummate his marriage. He slid his hand back and forth, imitating the act that she feared, letting her get used to having him in intimate contact with her, at least. He left her lips to suckle her bared breasts again, listening as her panting breaths came faster and faster. She pushed her tongue into his mouth, pressing her legs tightly together capturing his hand, his fingers to her.

"Preston, Preston, I think I can do it. I think I'm ready for more," she panted in his ear as she clutched at his shoulders, trying to get closer to him.

It didn't take Preston a second to lift her off the sofa and carry her into their room, which the ladies had readied earlier that morning with flowers and clean linen. The counterpane had been turned down for the loving couple. Setting Trudy on the bed, Preston pulled her gown off over her head then rolled down her stockings and covered her with the blanket so she didn't get chilled.

Pulling down his suspenders, Preston took off his shirt, then removed his shoes and undid his trousers. He was afraid that if Trudy saw his aroused body, she would shy away from him again. Then realized she had the right to see him, what making love entailed. Pushing down his trousers, he stepped out of them making sure she had time to see his entire body before he climbed into bed next to her.

Shivering, she didn't turn away, actually rolling toward his warmer body.

"I'll go slow and you can stop me any time, Darling," he whispered. They kissed. The passion still hot from their time on the sofa. He slid his hand back between her legs and he suckled on her ever-eager breasts. Soon she was panting with un-known wants.

Trudy seemed eager for his touch and he was having difficulty not going all the way, especially when she said she was ready. He was afraid that if she had a bad experience, she would close to him forever. He wished there was some other way, but as Trudy said, there was no way around it.

Preston covered Trudy, his erection poised between her legs as she pulled his hips to her, whispering, "I'm ready, it will be fine."

Praying she was right, he pushed into the warmth waiting for him, feeling her stiffen with the pain, but then joined his movements, signaling her eager participation with him, eagerly seeking the culmination she was unaware was a few moments away. Taking his time, Trudy was soon reaching her orgasm, sending Preston over the cliff with her, falling back to earth together, bathed in the euphoric afterglow.

"Oh, Preston, I'm so glad I said I wasn't afraid. I was, but I wanted to please you so badly. I didn't want to let you down, disappoint you," Trudy confessed while trying to catch her breath.

"Darling, you could never disappoint me, but I'm glad you took a chance with me today. We'll treasure this time together forever. I love you for always." He snuggled down with his wife in his arms. "Now go to sleep. There's more to making love but we'll need to rest first."

Andy and Walker arrived at their little house. They hadn't explained that this was their wedding day to their landlord but had simply said they were arriving after Trudy's wedding. This was Andy's first look at her home for the next few months which was longer than she had ever stayed anywhere in her life. Life with her father had been on the road, too.

The house was laid out much like Preston's only with an attic room set up as a bedroom, too. The furniture was older than Preston's, less carved and of lighter wood. The walls also had some paneling and all of it was painted, even the fireplace although the cookstove seemed to be the main source of heat. Other than a few mementos the son had removed upon his mother's death, everything was left in place, even dishes, flatware and linen.

Andy smiled her pleasure saying, "I think you did very well, and lucky to get it on such short notice. You're a good provider, Mr. Walker."

"That's nothing to what I can provide you with, Mrs. Walker," he bragged pulling her into his arms.

After kissing for several minutes, Andy took his hand and pulled him into the bedroom they were to use as their own. Helping him take off his suit coat and vest, she pushed her husband unto the bed. Pulling down his suspenders, she unbuttoned his shirt but Walker pulled it off over his head, too impatient to wait.

Smiling at him, Andy took her time hanging the coat and vest up properly, picking-up the shirt and placing it on the footstool in the corner. She bent and slipped off his boots grunting with the last tug. Then examined his trousers, figuring how to undo the buttons while he sat on the bed.

"I was waiting to see how far you were going to take this," Walker teased as he reached for her. "I think it's time I reciprocated the attention."

"Oh, so I stand here while you undress me? Is this how it goes usually?" She smiled back at her still grinning husband.

"No, it usually goes with you taking your clothes off to some slow sexy music, while I sit and watch, whistling when I see something I like," he told her seriously.

"Walker, you're making things up. You do remember that I've worked in gaming palaces, too, and such dancers were often located in or near some of the gaming tables. Really, you are such a bad man," she said, turning her back to him so that he could unbutton her gown.

To his delight, she swayed her hips as she began to pull her gown with its sewn in petticoats down to the floor stepping out of it. Standing in only her corset over her camisole and bustle tied around her waist she gave him a sassy wink. Turning her back to him again she wiggled her fanny much to his delight as his throat went dry and he licked his lips trying to moisten them.

The padded bustle dropped to the carpet followed by the corset that tied in front. Now there was simply a long camisole, which wasn't all that long, the brown thatch of hair showing between the tops of her stockings and the bottom of her covering.

Walker made a growl deep in his throat and lunged at Andy, hugging her to him as he kissed her thoroughly, making her giggle with his actions.

"I am done being teased. You have to pay a price for tempting me. Come here and take your punishment like a good wife."

Andy let Walker push her to the bed as he followed her down then turned onto his back. "You still have work to do, wife. I know you've felt this at your back before. Why don't you investigate what you've got as a husband?"

Andy rolled onto her side placing her hand at the opening of his trousers saying, "I've felt it more than just at my back. I've not been with you when you weren't in an interesting condition."

"Interesting, you call it? I'm in physical pain and you call it interesting?"

"Does it hurt?" She felt remorse for not knowing. "I didn't know. I could have done something to help you. Touch you or something," she offered, stroking the rigid member, sympathetic that he had been in pain. She pushed his trousers down and he wiggled out of them using his feet to push them off.

"That probably would have made it worse. I lived through it. I just seemed to be in a constant state of arousal and it gets to aching after a while." He kissed her mouth, sucking the lower lip into his. His tongue swiped between her lips, asking for permission to enter which she gave.

"Mmmm, Andy, love, I don't think I can play at this much longer. Parts of me want to get very, very serious with this. Are you ready for me?" he asked, pressing his palm to one of her breasts, his mouth on the other. Andy arched her body into Walker, allowing his mouth full access to every part of her.

His hand slid down her stomach and into the warm moistness waiting for any of his body parts, his finger finding and massaging the hidden nub. Andy caught her breath with the motion pressing her hips to his body, catching his hand between the two of them.

Pulling Walker onto her, he let his arousal lay on the nest of curls between her legs, his hands going to her breast as he took most of his weight on his elbows.

"I'm not sure I can do this, Andy. I know it's going to hurt. I need you to know ahead of time. I love you and I really want to make love with you, but I need to tell you it will hurt the first time I enter you."

"I know, Walker, Bea explained it to us. I'm ready

to have you make love to me," she said easily.

"Always so practical, my darling. I should have known you would do your homework before going into anything new. Tell me if it hurts too much or you want me to stop."

He kissed her as she opened for him, giving him room to slide between her legs as he entered her. Andy held her breath then exhaled as she realized he was encompassed inside her, filling her completely. The little bit of pain every woman feared was in the past.

The couple began the age-old dance of advancing and receding until both were breathing heavily, stretching for something that seemed just outside their reach until it wasn't. The orgasm was shared then doubled, both of them stiffening then shuddering to a peak. Andy's internal muscles clenched on Walker's erection as he made his last thrust. Their breathing began to return to a normal rhythm and Walker raised his head from leaning it against her neck.

"My God, honey, that was worth waiting for. I hope it didn't hurt too much. I was worried about that and had trouble focusing on anything else. I'll do better next time, I promise."

"Oh, Walker, if that gets any better, I'll need to limit your access to me." Andy chuckled out the compliment.

"You'll have a fight on your hands if you try to limit me now, honey. Am I forgiven for any sins I've ever committed?"

"So, you're trying to get me to give you free rein so to speak? Well, Mr. Walker, you have it. I am available for lovemaking any time you want. I understand that a man has to wait between sessions so let's sleep and we'll see if we can do it again tomorrow night."

"Wife, you are pushing me too far. I'll show you what a man can do, come here." And he began the whole process over again, his arousal the first to the party.

Devlin realized Bea hadn't rented the room when he went to find her later that day. Then trailed her to the train station once again. This time the porter and friendly ticket seller couldn't help him. A lot of people had come though the station that afternoon and if the ticket had been purchased on another day or from the conductor, they wouldn't be able to figure it out.

On top of it all, Devlin received his orders confirming that he and Walker should go after Clive Winters. This was a hell of a time for his superiors to finally figure out their priorities.

CHAPTER TWELVE

Walker and Devlin were on their fourth week of chasing the newly named Winter's gang, which had been laying low since the stagecoach robbery on the road to Lemmoxville. That had been typical of the gang, but Devlin couldn't help but think they had spooked Winter's in Coyote Gulch. Up till then, none of the gang had been identified and up till this last stagecoach, no one had been killed during one of their criminal acts, only wounded. Now there was only the noose waiting for any of the gang members caught.

Both men were grouchy, pretty much for the same reason.

"You haven't been worth a damn since you got married, Walker. That's why lawmen like us should remain bachelors. You can't keep your mind on the business at hand. You're dreaming about getting home and what you could be doing with that pretty little wife of yours," groused Devlin as he came to replace Walker on the stakeout.

"You're a great one to talk. Every tall woman gets a twice over to make sure it isn't Bea in disguise. I've never seen a man so besotted and so rigid he won't admit it, even to himself," countered Walker to his superior, pulling the tail of the tiger.

"I'm not besotted. I promised to find Mick for her and I'm working on it." Devlin found a comfortable position from which to watch the boardinghouse across the street.

"You're only following through on that promise because you think finding Mick will eventually lead you to Bea. You're a fool to think once she finds this Mick that she'll then be so grateful she'll fall into your arms. You'll find Mick for her and they'll ride off into the sunset together," prophesized Walker getting ready to leave to get a meal.

"I have my reasons for thinking otherwise." Then to get things back on track asked un-necessarily, "No new activity on Winter's brother?"

"No, still seems house-bound. Lots of visitors to the house though during the day. May be that the gang is beginning to get together. Clive's brother is supposedly up and walking now so there shouldn't be too much to hold the gang back. No idea of what the target is though," Walker told Devlin and then turned. "I'm off to grab a bite of food and return to my bed. See you next shift."

Devlin knew he was irritable. This on twelve-hours, off twelve-hours was getting to him and Walker. He couldn't blame Walker for wanting to get back to his new wife. After all, nothing was more boring than watching a man or a house when nothing seemed to be happening. But that was the point of a stakeout. Eventually something happened, and Devlin wanted to know when that occurred. Preferably before anyone else got hurt or killed.

Folding the paper over the tobacco, Devlin sealed it with his moist tongue. Pinching the edges together, he lit the cigarette letting the smoke spiral upwards into the night air. A stakeout was worse at night. Little happened at the boardinghouse and the cold made a man want to snuggle down into his coat and take a nap. Devlin, of course, didn't allow himself that luxury even if all the lights were now out in the watched building.

Devlin threw the cigarette to the ground and stepped on it, extinguishing the telltale red amber of the tip.

Focusing on the movement in the shadow, he discerned the shape of a man as he knocked lightly on the door, slipping into the interior darkness when the door opened. Because there were no lights on inside the boardinghouse, it was difficult to see who had opened the door let alone who entered.

Devlin was just about to go up to the windows to see if he could find any activity inside when the door opened again and the single man came out, now walking quickly away from the house towards the main streets.

"Gotcha, you bastard," whispered Devlin as he decided that following the shadow made more sense than watching a dark house.

In the morning, Walker found the space empty where he and Devlin had decided they could hide without being noticed. He looked towards the boarding house, which seemed to be as usual this time of day. He wondered where Devlin had got himself off to, but his orders were to watch the house so that's what he'd do until ordered to do otherwise or Winter showed up. He was the only man known to be from the gang so far. His brother's injury occurred right about the time the stage had been attacked. Possibly wounded during the robbery by one of the lawmen sent to protect it. Watching the brother made sense to get to Clive.

Walker heard a step a few yards behind him and turned, aiming his gun and pulling back the hammer at the same time only to face Devlin, his hands in the air.

"I didn't dare call out. I found Winter. He's got a room above a shoe shop over on Seventh near Oak. I think there may be a woman he's living with so we can't just rush in there, guns flaring. She may be completely innocent of the robberies and is only being used to get food and provisions, allowing Winter to stay hidden during the day."

"What's the plan then? Get Winter first and then come back for his brother before he gets wind of it and runs? He seems fit enough to ride if he had to," Walker said.

"I think that's the best sequence. Anything else and we might lose Winter again. I don't want to spend the whole winter freezing my ass off watching boardinghouses and saloons."

"Then we have a plan. Are you going to notify the local sheriff?"

"I'll tell him when I drop off Winter to the jail. I don't need a bunch of others in the way and possibly getting hit in a crossfire."

Walker nodded and they left together, hopefully to end this gang's activities once and for all.

When Devlin and Walker got to Seventh Street, Devlin told Walker, "Go into the alley and watch the store from the rear. Winter might try to jump from the second story and escape as I come though the stairway in front."

And that was exactly how it went down from Walker's viewpoint.

Winter jumped from the window, leaving his girlfriend to keep Devlin occupied. On landing, he sprained his ankle and Walker had no trouble in wrestling Winter's gun from his hand.

"You're lucky you didn't shoot yourself jumping from a window with a loaded gun in your hand. It's amazing you don't have more damage done to yourself," Walker said as he pulled Winter over unto his stomach securing his hands behind his back with manacles.

"Go screw yourself, lawman. I'm not saying anything," Winter said with bravado.

"Don't need you to. We seem to have your woman who I can hear doesn't want to hang for being part of several killings. We have a witness to your murder of two Pinkertons and will be rounding-up your brother as soon as we dump you off. I'd say your gang is in immediate danger of being hauled to justice." Walker tugged the now harmless criminal to his feet.

He dragged the limping man to the street front where Devlin was pulling out the woman who knew no bounds when it came to talking to save her own ass. She was giving dates and names and places so quickly Walker was hoping Devlin could keep up with it all.

Devlin called out, "I've sent the son of the shoemaker to fetch the Black Maria for these two. The dynamite and some other things are upstairs for the next job, a train robbery this time. They were waiting for Winter's brother to heal. Seems like he's the sharp-shooter of the group. Likes to pick off the main guards or, in this instance, the engineer so the rest of the gang can get the gold."

"You got all that in this short of time? You're right, she is a talker," laughed Walker, riding on the adrenalin rush of capturing a man they had been after for so long.

Local deputies arrived with the police wagon and took the two into custody, knowing the seriousness of their crimes and thusly the amount and danger they would go to, to escape.

Devlin and Walker picked-up Winter's brother who was taken into custody easily along with another member of the gang the landlady pointed out, angry and affronted they had used her boardinghouse to lay low for the past few months. That man worked for the stagecoach line.

Finally, the two federal lawmen found themselves on the train to Lemmoxville.

Devlin, pulling his hat low over his eyes leaned back telling his deputy, "If I were you, I'd try to get a little shut-eye, too. You've got a new bride waiting for you and you wouldn't want to disappoint her."

"I never disappoint her," Walker claimed but took the advice and leaned back covering his eyes with his own hat. The problem was, though, all he could see was Andy doing that strip tease for him on their wedding night, which kept him awake and up most of the trip home.

CHAPTER THIRTEEN

Devlin and Walker studied the map with all the towns marked that Bea and the twins lived in for the past two years, before crossing the Texas border. Andy didn't want to help the men find Bea, at first, but her oldest sister hadn't been heard from since a brief note arrived at Andy's door after the weddings.

Apologizing for not saying a proper goodbye, Bea explained she didn't want to dampen their wedding day with a long goodbye. Now Andy and Trudy both were worried knowing how dangerous some of the towns were and the places Bea would work to get money and information trying to locate Mick.

"If you see, there's a pattern here that follows the poker circuit. Each town, less a few months of the girls getting there, was home to a big game." His finger touched several spots on the map. "Here it was the cattle round-up, here was a contest put on by the largest casino group in the state. These were qualifying rounds but too small for Mick to be interested in," Devlin said pointing to the red dots on the map. "He goes with the money, the big money and the big players. He pits himself against the best. All I have to do is keep track of these gambling events and I'll run smack into him and maybe, Bea, at the same time."

Walker nodded, seeing the pattern himself now. "So instead of following his path like Bea was doing you're going to meet him at the tables."

"That's the plan although he doesn't seem to have done anything illegal that I've heard about. The mining claim was part of a winning hand and he travelled to Coyote Gulch to see it firsthand and sell it off. He never planned on working it. Too hard on a gambler's hands," Devlin said with a little spite.

Andy said worriedly, "I just want to know she's all right. Tell her to write to us so we know where she is and that she's still safe. I don't want you to drag her back here, Devlin. I don't want her hurt."

"I won't hurt her. What do you think, I am? I'll find her and tell her to contact you. A visit wouldn't be out of the question, though. You and Trudy are both worried and it's selfish of her to ignore you to go traipsing after this Mick," Devlin told his friend's wife.

"Maybe, but we know she loves us, too," Andy said not trying to be unkind to Devlin reminding him that Bea loved Mick and might not ever want to come back if she found him. "Now come to supper, the food is going to get cold."

Devlin had been a regular guest at either Andy or Trudy's many nights of the week when he was in town and not on assignment. He rented part of a house in the same neighborhood so it seemed churlish to turn down the hospitality, plus being around the twins made him less lonely, miss Bea a little less. He liked to hear about their life before he found Bea working in that casino with Maurice. The many jobs, the many rooms.

He didn't like to hear about the close calls Bea got into but then out of. When Preston met Trudy that had been the first time that twin had worked in a casino or any kind of gaming hall. Bea usually took that lead position. Devlin felt a little guilty about that since it was his pursuit of Bea that had her trying to lay-low. He took solace in the fact it might have brought Preston and Trudy together quicker, brought out Preston's need to protect Trudy.

Leaving Walker's house, Devlin strolled down through the snow-dusted walks. He was wondering where Bea was and if she was wearing warm clothes, if she was eating properly now that she wasn't having meals with the twins. Whether she ever thought of him in any way besides with relief she didn't need to deal with him any longer.

Feeling sorry for himself, he thought, *I'm going to find that woman before I go crazy with worry. Bea had a lot to answer for, leaving us here not knowing where she went or if she was safe.* Devlin reached home at record speed, stomping through the snow leaving prints several feet apart.

The pounding on the door woke Devlin to a headache he wasn't aware he had. He pulled on his trousers, leaving the suspenders hanging, his cocked gun in his hand and met a flustered Trudy on his porch, a letter in her hand.

"Bea wrote. She's says she's fine and that we are not to worry. It's been cold but she has a nice warm room and nice people around her," Trudy relayed the letter's contents, and then smiled in relief. "I think she's being honest with us. I'm to share the letter she said."

"With me?" Devlin asked doubtfully.

"Well, not exactly but she didn't say not to share it with you. I already read it to Andy and Walker, but he thought you would want to hear about it right away, too," Trudy told him as he perused the letter, noting there wasn't a return address only a postmark that didn't make sense. It was hundreds of miles from the next town Devlin thought Mick would be in.

"I appreciate you bringing it. I'm glad she finally wrote to let you know she's safe. We'll have to celebrate or something when I get back to town."

"Oh, are you and Walker out on assignment again so soon? It seems like you just returned," Trudy said sadly. "I know whenever Walker is on assignment, Andy worries and frets until he's back. That's why I feel so lucky to be married to a Pinkerton."

"No, this time they're only sending me. Walker earned his time off after having to leave without a honeymoon. I'll keep in touch if I learn anything about Bea," he said as Trudy left through the still un-swept snow on his front path. It would probably melt by the afternoon since it never stayed long in this part of Texas.

Devlin watched as Trudy headed for home and then slammed his door closed, knowing the letter was a lie, a cover. Bea was too eager to answer all her sisters' worries. She's safe, warm room, nice people around her. Like hell! She's trying to make sure the twins don't send their husbands after her. Well, he wasn't fooled and he knew she wasn't in the town on that postmark.

He was going to go to the next town the map indicated Mick would be in and wait there until either he found Mick or he found Bea.

Devlin rubbed his gloved hands together, thinking this had to be the coldest day of the year so far. Not much snow, but bone chilling winds that froze over the water in the horse troughs and formed frost on every windowpane. He had spent every night searching the casinos and gaming halls, but no one seemed to remember a tall redhead. Devlin supposed she could have dyed her hair, but she never had before and the same for bleaching. A worry nagged at hm. Bea had never been trying to hide from someone before and he was a trained lawman so she might go to those lengths this time.

He would get a bite to eat and then visit a few less popular gaming halls this evening, hoping someone would remember seeing her even if she was gone now. She might not have realized what Mick was doing and was still following him. But Bea was smart, she would have seen the pattern as he had once Mick had been in the state long enough.

His head was crouched down into the collar of his sheepskin coat when he caught a flash of something out of the corner of his eye in a shop window. It was a re-sale shop for women's clothes. Gowns and dresses mostly from women who wore gowns once and then disposed of them not wanting to be seen twice in the same garment.

There in the window was a very familiar green dress. Bea's, he would know it anywhere. The low-scooped neckline making him remember the white swell of her breasts as she dealt hand after hand of Black Jack.

Stepping into the store, he was met by a woman with a faux French accent.

"Monsieur, how can I be of service?" her large brown eyes looked him up and down trying to estimate his purchasing power.

"I'm interested in that green gown in the window. What can you tell me about it?"

"It is of extremely high quality in both the materials and style, with the scooped neck and Irish lace, the waterfall bustle…." The shop owner began explaining the reason for the high price she was going to ask for the gown when she was interrupted.

"No, I mean about the woman who brought it in," he said still gazing around the shop and its many gowns and shoes.

"Oh, mademoiselle is no longer in need of this gown." In a conspiratorially tone added, "I think she finds herself in a little financial difficulty or she would not have sold this lovely gown, *n'est-ce pas*?"

"A tall redhead?" Devlin asked.

The woman immediate saw her sale go out the window and replied with a mid-west accent. "I don't want to get anyone in trouble so if you're a scorned husband or lover, just keep moving. I don't disclose anything about my clients."

Devlin took the badge out of his pocket and slid it onto his coat, then said, "Was she a tall redhead and when did she bring in this gown?"

Defeated, the proprietress answered, "Yes, she was a tall redhead. Who else could carry off a gown of that color? She first came here about a month ago, I guess. Said she had no use for it anymore."

"You said when she first came here. So, she's been here since?" Devlin asked honing in on what may have been a slip of the tongue.

"About a week later. She brought in this gown, too." She pulled out the gold brocade that Devlin had admired on Bea in Lemmoxville. "I couldn't resist it since it is of the same high quality."

"I'll take them both." He took out a wad of bills. "Did she walk or take a cab?" he asked knowing this woman would note how her customers arrived.

As she bundled and wrapped the gowns in paper, the proprietress said, "Walked. I've seen her over at the restaurant on the corner of Minton and Broadway. About three blocks east." Now that he was a customer, she was much more accommodating. Devlin thought he should have pulled out his wallet sooner and made this conversation much shorter.

Leaving with the package under his arm, he headed east, hoping his luck would last and he would spot Bea going into the restaurant or walking on the sidewalk. He reached the restaurant and entered, finding a table where he could face the door and front window. The waiter came and took his order, but Devlin's attention was on what was happening outside, not on what he was going to eat. He doubted he was going to taste it anyways, his excitement at being this close to his quarry making his mouth go dry.

Luck was not with him, or rather, it was with Bea. There was no sign of her and although the waiter knew of the lovely redhead, he said it had been over a week since she had been in. When she did come in it was to order the simplest of meals. Devlin swore under his breath. That probably meant she was back to skipping meals to make her money last and if she was selling her gowns, she couldn't have a job at a casino. Maybe all she could get this time was a lower wage job like the one she had cooking and waitressing in Lemmoxville.

Devlin didn't waste his time searching in the casinos but set up a grid to check the neighborhood that encompassed the restaurant and the dress shop. He went to sleep early wanting to be on the streets at daybreak hoping to catch Bea going to work and asking others if they had seen the tall beauty.

It was almost midday, when Devlin finally found a shopkeeper who remembered seeing a tall woman who possibly had red hair. But she was a widow and still wore the black veil of mourning. Devlin smiled that 'I got'cha' smile and thanked the man who he had stopped from going to his noonday meal.

He would narrow the search to fewer blocks, getting it down to just a couple now, and wondering what she was up to, wearing widow garb. Did she think he wouldn't discover her disguise? Besides, she had tried that once before and he had found her. Bea was running out of ideas it seemed.

The next day, Devlin just about whooped with joy when he saw a widow dressed in black, including the veil. She had a gray cape wrapped around her as she walked against the wind. But Devlin knew it was Bea, could tell from how she held herself when the wind allowed her to stand straight, from the way she floated along the brick sidewalk. He trailed her to see if she would lead him to her home. That way he would know where to find her if she didn't go back with him to let her sisters know she was all right.

Following her to a church, he watched as she opened the annex door without hesitation, evidently quite used to being there. Devlin followed her and found a large room filled with cast-off clothing and dishes, shoes and curtains. He went closer to the front of the room and saw the minister, wearing the cleric's collar and a wide smile on his face as he and Bea conversed over a pile in front of her on a table.

Devlin watched Bea from the back as she bent and picked up a doily and then he could hear the two people speaking.

"I can take these home with me and fix the needle point where it's missing. And I can crochet an edge on this pillow slip and it will sell for much more than a plain one will."

"Oh, thank you Mrs. Crest, that is so kind of you.

The rummage sale is our big money maker for the year and we need to make the most of the donations we have," the cleric said letting his hand touch Bea's as he handed her another item in need of mending.

So, that's the way the wind blows thought Devlin. The minister would like to be a lot closer than her spiritual guide.

As Bea turned sideways, Devlin saw her full silhouette and the world dropped away from under his feet. Bea was with child, his child. That's why she wasn't needing her gowns. She was too large to work at a casino and the widow's weeds were to cover the fact she didn't have a wedding ring, at least, not a legitimate wedding ring.

Without hesitating, Devlin was going to burn her bridges. Striding up to the couple and ignoring the other women sorting and cleaning the donated items, Devlin flashed his badge and announced, "Miss Taylor, you are under arrest for fraud. I'm taking you into custody. Put out your hands."

Bea gasped in surprise and tried to formulate a response while she put her hands in front of her unconsciously obeying his command as he slipped the manacles over her leather gloves.

The cleric, his face red with emotion, said, "There must be some mistake, this is Mrs. Crest. She's been a member with us for months now."

"She is Miss Taylor and I've been following her for months and finally caught up with her. She spins plausible tales wherever she goes, being helpful and worming her way into a community. She probably had her eye on the church funds, waiting until after this sale to make the big haul," Devlin fabricated as he went.

"She's not even with child. Turns her bustle around backwards just to appear as if she is."

The cleric jumped back from Bea as if burned and then doubt came into his eyes. "I thought how helpful she was. She told me she was bored and had nothing else to occupy her time while waiting for the baby to be born."

Bea said, gritting her teeth in impotent rage, "You are the devil! Let me go this instant, Devil!"

Then the cleric took hold of his cross and stared at both Bea and Devlin as if he thought he needed to call in the bishop for an exorcism.

Devlin almost laughed but had his hands full of Bea as she began to resist his trying to remove her from the building. Finally, fearing she may do something to hurt the baby, he swung her up into his arms and carried her out the door, which had been opened by an obliging church member.

"I will hate you for the rest of my life, Devil. How dare you lie. I could have your badge for this," she said furiously as he continued to stride down the street. He wasn't sure where he was going but then he hadn't expected to find her carrying his child either.

"Doesn't matter, I'll tell them I got the wrong woman by error. They'll warn me to be more careful and apologize to you for any inconvenience," he told her not out of breath with his exertion.

"But I am inconvenienced, very inconvenienced, Devil. I want down now. We are causing a scene and I don't want to be kicked out of my rooming house. I only got in there because I told them I was a new widow and in mourning," Bea said. He knew she was hoping he would put her down before they reached the block she lived on.

"Are you sure you won't try to run? It can't be good for the baby," he said letting his hand rub over her stomach as he placed her feet on the sidewalk in front of him.

"I don't understand your concern now. You certainly didn't show me any when you were impregnating me," Bea said coarsely, letting the venom that had been building in her spill out all over its intended target.

It hit the mark and Devlin said quietly, "I'm sorry for not protecting you. I'm usually very careful about such things."

"Well, I can't find too much comfort in that now, can I? All the other women you were with, you were more careful of than me." Finally seeming tired of their verbal sparring, she said, "I need to sit down, Devil. I can't simply stand out here in the street."

"I can't just leave you here, not that I was going to. We need to talk this out, Bea. You should have told me," he said softly, sorry they had gotten off on such a bad footing with this meeting.

"I don't care what you want, Devil. I don't need you. I can make this on my own, just don't tell the twins. When it's over, after I have the baby, then I'll tell them," she said, looking anywhere but at the man standing next to her, holding her arm not trusting her not to run.

"Bea, you don't know how much this has affected me, seeing you again and then finding you carrying my child." He tried to explain all the protective and possessive feelings rolling through him. How the plans he had for them was altering into marriage and a home and siblings for this child. That he had been fooling himself if he ever thought it to be less than that. A man…Devlin, didn't chase after a one-night-stand or two if he remembered the night on the trail and he did. He did almost every night.

"It's not your…." she began.

Devlin stopped her saying, "Don't say those hurtful words. Don't lie about the father of this child."

Tears came to her eyes and she wiped them away with her gloves. Devlin handed her a clean handkerchief, which she proceeded to soak.

So much for trying to be helpful Devlin thought. "Come on, Red. You need something to warm you up."

Bea walked beside him, trying to keep-up with his wide steps until he realized that she was practically running and he slowed leading her to the restaurant.

"Do you have that pot roast today?" he asked the waiter as he led Bea to his table.

"Yes, sir, made fresh daily," the waiter answered.

"We'll have coffee." At Bea's squeak and her hand to her mouth Devlin squinted at her. "I'll have coffee and the lady will have a pot of tea. Pot roast for both of us with plenty of potatoes and carrots," Devlin told the waiter.

Bea sat quietly in the chair. She acknowledged the pot of tea and stirred sugar into the hot brew before taking careful sips. Devlin watched her, taking in every movement, every grimace from the hot tea, loving the feeling of being near her again.

When the food came, he relished the speed that Bea began eating, taking a neat little bite full, chewing and swallowing, and then another neat little bite full ignoring him completely.

"You haven't been eating again," he stated, not a

question.

"I got used to not eating much when I had the morning sickness but then it got better. I still can't drink coffee." She glared at his cup as if it were a viper.

"Does the smell bother you? I can have the waiter take it away," he offered trying to placate her in any way he could.

"No, I'm fine. It isn't pretty when I'm not," she said, almost smiling. "Thank you for the meal. Tell the twins I love them and will be back to see them in a few months."

"Is that when the baby will be born?" he asked innocently.

Bea glared at him and said icily, "I thought you said you knew it was your child. Now you're questioning the timing?"

"No, I know when we made love. What I don't know is how long it takes, you know, for the baby to be ready to be born," he said uncomfortably. "Are you planning on keeping it?"

Bea shot to her feet, her face red with anger. "What do you think of me? Why do you keep following me and ruining my life? If you had left me alone, none of this would even be happening. I have a plan and I am following it. It did not, however, include you or your interfering with it. I will now have to move once again and start all over."

"Bea, sit down and listen," he said trying to calm the woman who was beginning to appear unwell. "You're too tired to think this through right now. Let me take you where you can rest."

"Back to my room? Can I go back to my room now?" she asked, her shoulders drooping with the fatigue that was beginning to be her focus.

Devlin helped her into her cape and shoved her gloves into his pocket, "Come on, Red, let's get a cab and go to my room. Then we can talk after you rest."

Bea went uncomplaining with Devlin, the tiredness that kept overtaking her each afternoon so overwhelming she simply wanted a place to lay her head. Devlin flagged down a cab, helped her take a seat and gave the address of his hotel. When they got there, Devlin handed over the fare and helped Bea to the door then into the hotel's lobby stopping at the front desk.

"My wife has gotten here earlier than I had expected," he informed the front desk manager who eyed the gold band on Bea's hand. "We'll be checking out in the morning."

"Certainly, sir. I will have the bill ready for you. If there is anything you or your wife may need please let me know," the thin man informed the couple.

Bea hadn't taken notice of everything being said. She was so tired she didn't care anymore.

"Come on, Red, it's bed, for you." He helped her up the stairs to his room. Bea barely noticed the large room except for the lace curtains and white counterpane. Bea only saw the bed as she swayed with fatigue.

Removing her cape, Devlin turned her to undo the buttons down the back and pulled the dress up over her head, leaving her in her camisole and pantaloons for warmth, the need for a bustle or petticoats gone until Bea's figure returned.

He lost his breath as he gazed on the bulge that kept his child warm and protected and then helped Bea into the bed, covering her with the thick comforter. She was asleep almost immediately. Devlin kissed her forehead and went to make himself comfortable in the larger chair, propping one of the pillows behind his head to take a nap. The talk he and Bea needed to have could wait, everything could wait, as long as she was with him.

A few hours later Bea woke up and moaned as she stretched.

Devlin was up and awake immediately. "Are you in pain? Can I get you something?" he asked going to the side of the bed.

"You undressed me," she accused him.

He laughed at her indignation and said, "Just the outside bits, Red. Nothing I haven't seen before."

"I don't care. That was a long time ago. I've never given you the right to remove my clothing," she said searching for her dress while holding the cover up over her breasts.

"Well, that may mean I can talk to you now. Do you want me to order some tea or soup or anything?" he offered before he began the conversation that was probably going to end in a row.

"I have a plan. I can simply start over in another town," she explained bluntly, no chance of changing her mind.

"You were never able to tell me when the baby is due to be born and if you were planning on keeping it. If not, as the father, I would accept full responsibility and adopt the child, taking him to live in my home in Aberdeen. My mother is more than capable of caring for a child," he told her letting this information sink in.

"How dare you make plans for my child, a child you had no idea you even fathered until today. I'm the one who went through weeks of morning sickness that, by the way, lasts all day, loss of sleep and now total fatigue. And I'm hungry all the time." Tears began to run down her face, making Devlin feel like the scum of the earth.

"Can I come and sit by you on the bed, just sit there Red, nothing more," he asked, pleading with his eyes. Wanting to hold her and give her comfort after her having been alone for so long.

Nodding, she moved over to give him room and he pulled her to him, letting her rest against his chest as he said, "Red, let me help you. I don't want to take the baby from you, the most important person in a child's life is their mother. I want to be the mother's main support, monetarily, physically and emotionally. You're tired and need someone to help with the day to day things. I'll make sure you won't need to worry about anything. It's what I should have been doing all along."

"I have a plan. I was to be a widow, left carrying a child. I would have that child then after a few months find a nursemaid for the baby and I could return to work. I can make good money in the right casino," she told him rationally.

"And when did you think you were going to see the child? Working all night and sleeping most of the day? I'm not sure you've looked at this unemotionally. Let me take on the financial burden for you, at least. Come home so the twins can pamper you and coo over their niece or nephew," he cajoled, hoping his plan would be the one followed. He needed to get her home to her sisters so he had a chance of convincing her he belonged in her plans, too.

"But they'll never let me leave again. I'll never find Mick," she said sadly.

Devlin's heart took a dive as he realized Mick was

still on the top of her mind, her one thought focused on this man who had consumed most of her adult life.

"You can begin again later. In fact, I thought you were here to meet up with him when the contest begins in a couple of weeks," he said, armoring his heart from this woman who was so in love with another man, she endangered herself and his child.

"You figured it out then, too. I finally got tired of following him and now I'm waiting for him to come to me. I thought it was going to happen this time. That we were going to see each other. I knew he'd be shocked that I'm with child, but he had to know I would grow and change too, just as he has, I'm sure." She leaned against Devlin's chest as if listening to the rumbling of his voice through his body.

"If I promise you that I will return here to the gaming and bring Mick back to you, even if I need to arrest him, will you come back with me? Let me care for you and my child?" He held his breath for her answer because if it was, no, he wasn't sure what he would be able to do. She had all the power and he felt impotent to do anything of substance.

"It's my child, Devlin, I'm having a child. You planted a seed and some days I'm very grateful for that seed as I will be once my child is born. But you didn't mean to father a child, you merely got carried away one night on the trail and forgot to use protection. I don't hold you accountable and I don't want your money," she stated plainly letting him know he could walk away freely.

"I hold myself accountable. When I saw you today and you were so obviously big with my child, I knew I was going to need to fight for you both. I won't leave you here. If there were complications or if you became sick and couldn't get to food or medical care…." He found himself unable to continue and instead finished, "I can't leave you alone, Red. I'm here to stay if you won't return to Lemmoxville."

"I can't inflict myself on either of my sisters who, as you know, are newlyweds, married only a few months. They don't need a gooseberry hanging around all day," Bea said reasonably.

"I was thinking more of you staying with me, in my house which is near both your sister's homes. I would marry you but wouldn't expect any husbandly rights. Simply the right to take care of you and the child. If, later, you want a divorce, if you and Mick decide to move on together, then I wouldn't fight it." Devlin hoped his voice didn't waver with the emotion it took for him to tell her she could leave him for Mick if she desired the other man more.

"I don't know, Devlin, that doesn't sound like a good reason to get married," she said doubtfully.

"You carrying my child should be reason enough. This child needs a last name, a birthright and I want to give him or her that," he assured her, his thumb rubbing her arm where he held her.

"I don't want to impose the name of bastard to this child, Devlin, but I'm not marriage material, yet. I'm still searching for Mick and I need to see him again before I can go on with the rest of my life."

"I'm not sure anyone would say I was marriage material either, but this isn't about us, is it? This child needs the best we can offer. I'm more than ready to place myself in your hands to give this baby both a mother and father when it's born."

He kissed Bea on the shoulder, finishing, "I promise to take good care of you both for as long as you'll let me."

Bea was never sure after that if she had agreed to marriage or if she was simply too tired to come up with any more reasons not to. She remembered being offered a dinner, room service, but she mumbled she was too full from the midday meal and the next thing she knew she was waking up beside Devlin, who was wearing a full union suit and a day's growth of beard.

"Morning, Red. You ready to go and pack up your things? I sent a wire and your sisters will be waiting at the station to welcome you home, I'm sure." He swung his long legs off the bed.

Although they had been intimate, they had never lived intimately. She was embarrassed to be in his bed wearing little more than what was descent and had to decide if she was going to return with him as he supposed. If she packed quickly, she could get somewhere and stay hidden for a while until he became tired of waiting or got called to an assignment.

"I see the wheels turning, Red. We have an agreement and I mean to have us stick to it. You need me for the next few months. It's going to be a long cold winter. Now get dressed. The water closet is down the hall and I ordered an early breakfast," he told her lathering up his face at the washstand.

It had been years since she had watched Mick shave. Amazed that Devlin didn't cut off his nose with the sharp little blade. He shaved with accuracy and speed. The same way he did everything else. Bea shook her head to clear the image and got up to grab her clothes Devlin had placed on the end of her bed.

Breakfast came and Bea wolfed down the poached eggs and toast, and then nibbled on the crisp bacon while Devlin watched with a crooked grin on his face, drinking his coffee after eating four eggs and a large slice of ham.

Bea became conscious of his attention as she wiped her mouth. "I'm sorry, there are times I get so hungry I forget good manners."

"Don't apologize, Red, it can't be easy growing a whole new person." He sipped from his cup again.

"Well, I don't suppose it's going to be a very big person to start with," she answered smiling, consciously placing her hand over her stomach.

Setting his cup down, Devlin said briskly before he took Bea to that big empty bed and made love to her, "We'll go and pack up your belongings and get to the station in time for the early train. I want to be back yet today."

The packing at the rooming house didn't take long. The older women who owned the house glared rudely at Bea as she walked past to get to her room. By the time Bea was done and carrying the bag out, which Devlin took from her immediately, the older woman was all smiles and well wishes.

Once back in the cab, Bea asked, "What did you say to her? When I first got there, she looked at me with complete disdain."

"I explained I had come to collect my wife after having an argument which was entirely my fault, but in your condition, took it to heart and left me," he told Bea then added, "And I paid her for the rest of the month and she became all pleasant innkeeper."

"I don't like that you lied merely to save face," she said angrily. "I rented by the week and she was paid through to the end. No wonder she was so smiley."

Devlin pulled her closer to his side, smiling that he had his family back together. He didn't give a damn what some old biddy thought of him, but he wasn't going to let Bea feel cheapened by anyone.

CHAPTER FOURTEEN

The train pulled to a stop, the steam making it impossible to see out the windows to the platform. Although it had only been a few months, Bea missed the twins immensely and now couldn't wait to catch up on what the newlyweds were doing in their lives. She hurried to the exit steps and Devlin followed carrying their two bags and a paper wrapped package.

As soon as her foot touched the platform, she heard the squeals and knew both twins were there, somewhere. Moving with the disembarking crowd, she was soon grabbed and hugged by Trudy who then stepped back and gazed in horror at Bea.

"Oh, Bea, you're having a baby and you never said a word." Tears formed in her blue eyes as she covered her quivering lips with her hand. Preston came up behind her, his eyes hard and dark as he stared daggers at Devlin.

Bea appeared uncertain, of anything she feared, having the twins turn away from her never entered her mind.

"Oh, that is wonderful, Bea. You're making us aunts. It will be so fun to help you get ready for the baby. When is it due? Do we have time to sew a proper layette or not?" Andy said hugging her older sister as if she might run without the anchor. "We can do the basics and then add to it as the baby grows. Oh, this is going to be so much fun. The three of us together again."

By the time Andy finished, Trudy had recovered from the shock and added, "I have a new sewing machine. It will make hemming the blankets and sewing the frocking so much easier. I can't wait to show it to you, Bea. We missed you terribly." She hugged her sister this time leaving room for the bulge protruding from the open cape.

Devlin ignored the dark glares from both men and asked Walker, "Did you get everything done I asked for in the wire?"

"Yes, the minister's been informed and understands there was a need for expediency," Walker answered, not happy with the condition of his sister-in-law and the implications that Devlin took advantage of his office to compromise Bea. That this was the reason Bea had disappeared when she did and not due to chasing off after Mick.

Walker turned to Bea saying, "If this isn't what you want, you're welcome to come live with us until you want to be back on your own. There's a room for you and the baby. We'll be there for anything you need."

Devlin stared at his friend in disbelief. Walker was standing there offering an alternative to Bea, one that excluded him completely. Before Devlin could argue that Bea was going to be taken care of, Bea spoke up.

"I am quite agreeable with the arrangements Devlin has made but thank you. I will appreciate having my sisters be a part of this child's life, to be the family it so rightly deserves," she said with a calm smile.

"Well, then it's on to the church," said Devlin, restraining his impatience with the time spent on the platform. She knew he feared as the minutes passed, she could have a change of heart despite her last comment.

The group found two cabs and again en masse headed to the church the twins were married in with the same older, kindly minister and his wife. Neither of which mentioned by look or word the bride's condition.

When it came time for Devlin to pledge his vows,

Bea felt terribly moved, nearly to tears. He held her hand and recited, without prompting, "With this ring I Thee wed, with my body I Thee worship, and with all my worldly goods I Thee endow, in the name of the Father, and the Son and of the Holy Ghost." Then he placed the wide gold band on her finger to take the place of the one she had removed in the cab.

Leaning down, he placed a chaste kiss on her lips then turned, a triumphant expression on his face. "Thank you for making this happen for us. A little past time, but in time. I know Bea is tired so if we can wait to celebrate in a day or two, we would appreciate it."

Bea tried to keep the smile in place knowing Devlin was right but unsure she could let someone else always speak for her, as if she suddenly became unable or feeble minded with this pregnancy. Everyone else nodded and put on their coats and capes and all three couples walked home quietly, unsure how they felt about the wedding that had just taken place.

Even the bride…especially the bride. What she knew was the best thing for her child was not necessarily the best thing for her. But as Devlin kept reminding her, she could get a divorce if or when the time came to separate herself from the father of her child.

Devlin held her arm in the crook of his as they walked the few blocks to his house.

"Here we are, Red. I didn't have much time to get furniture and such, but feel free to add whatever you think we need. I've never been good at the fluffy sort of stuff," he said as he pushed open the door to a warm parlor. "Walker must have been here today to make sure it was welcoming for you."

She entered a parlor and glanced over the sofa and

three matching chairs. There was an Axminster carpet on the floor and lace curtains on the windows. Three side tables and two matching oil lamps made up the rest of the furnishings. As she walked through the room, she saw there was an empty dining room, a partially equipped kitchen and two bedrooms with a water closet and bathing room between.

"It's very nice, Devlin. Everything we should need. What did Walker hand you at the station?"

"You saw that, did you? Just our next assignment. We need to leave tomorrow morning. Not the best timing. I could probably tell them to send someone else." He sounded hopeful she wanted him to stay. That she might miss him when he left.

"That's all right. The twins will keep me busy and Preston is here if I need anything." She covered her mouth when she yawned. "Do you mind if I rest now? Which room is to be mine?" she asked innocently.

Devlin's heart dropped. Bea wasn't going to think of this marriage as anything but something to protect her child's, their child's, good name. Their child, his child, will have the name of Devlin and they won't be able to change that. He was part of this child and this child was a part of him. That was enough to go on for now.

"I sleep in the front one," he told her noncommittally, and watched her go into the other.

In the early hours of the morning, Devlin came in to kiss his warm sleepy wife goodbye. "I left some money on the table. If you need more, get it from Preston and I'll pay him back. I laid out some things on the table for your breakfast. You slept through dinner again last night. Remember you're eating for two, don't skip meals. And

I'd like you to find a doctor or midwife or whatever to help you through the birth."

"Yes, Mother," she said sleepily, teasing him for being so bossy.

"I'm glad I'm not your mother. Your antics would have turned my hair gray," he teased back not wanting to leave her in the dark room, in the warm bed alone.

"Surprise for you Devil, you've got gray hair. You just don't look for them but they're there," she mumbled into the blanket.

"I'm lucky I have any hair left after what you've put me through. I'll be back in a week unless we need to stay. I'll send a wire to let you know," he said with one last kiss on her mouth.

"Devlin," she said just as he opened the door to leave so he stopped and waited, "have a safe trip, you and Walker."

"We will," he answered and left quickly before he changed his mind. How does Walker do it? Leave his wife when the orders come in like this? Maybe he was a stronger man than Devlin because he certainly wanted to march right back in to Bea and stay forever.

Bea was up, dressed and had made her bed when she went into Devlin's room. The bed was made and everything was neatly put away, even his shaving gear. The rest of the house was in about the same condition, sparse as Devlin had said, but also clean. It was like he didn't want to leave evidence of his ever being anywhere.

There was a rapping on the front door and both Andy and Trudy stood there, their arms full and baskets hanging from their hands. They came in excitedly, both talking at once. Trudy bubbling and Andy more prosaic.

"I brought us food and tea since I didn't think a bachelor would have enough of either," Andy, the ever practical, said.

Trudy began to pull material out of a paper bundle saying, "I thought this would be perfect for receiving blankets. I bought diaper material, too, but I plan on sewing those at home on the machine. Come feel this yarn, it's cashmere and so soft. I got the directions for crocheting a blanket so I thought one of us could start on that."

Bea became excited because her sisters were excited. No recriminations for leaving them without notice, no pouting or aggrieving. "It is all so lovely, when did you do all this?"

"Oh, we left right after Walker did and then bought out the store, well, not really, but we bought some of everything," Andy told her older sister, still taking items out of the basket and placing them on the kitchen table.

"Let me pay you back. Devlin left me money for anything I want," said Bea amazed at the growing pile of items for the baby.

"No," chimed younger sisters.

"This is our gift to our niece or nephew and, we hope, Godchild," said Trudy ungrammatically.

"I haven't even thought that far ahead. It was like I knew I was expecting but if I didn't acknowledge it, I wouldn't have to face the truth," Bea tried to explain.

Trudy went to Bea's side putting her arm around her saying, "We're here to help with anything. I'm sorry you felt you needed to leave rather than tell us. I mean, about you and Devlin."

Andy stood straighter and asked, "It happened on the trail, didn't it? We both wanted to be close to our men. That left you with Devlin and he wasn't the gentleman that Walker and Preston were. We caused this to happen and I'm so sorry, so very sorry."

Tears were in Trudy's eyes as she said looking at her older sister, "Oh, I never thought about that. I'm so sorry, too. Why didn't we think what we were doing that night?"

"It didn't happen that night," she told her sisters although she knew instinctively that it had. "I spent a night, well, part of a night with him in his hotel room before we left for Coyote Gulch."

"So, I didn't mistake your antagonism on the trail. I thought perhaps it was because he was forcing you into a relationship you didn't want," Andy said. Bea could see the wheels turning in her younger sister's mind. Andy would never leave anything incomplete. She would worry it to pieces until she understood every nuance.

"In a way, perhaps he was. You know I want to find Mick, give him a chance to stay now that we're older and things have changed." She placed her hand on her stomach. "I still plan on following after Mick. Devlin promised me he would help after the baby is born. Maybe sooner, going back to the town I was recently in when the contest starts in a couple of weeks. Mick's sure to show up there, it's one of the highest stake games this winter."

"Well, Devlin seems like a more understanding husband than Preston. Not to say he's strict or anything, but I'm prohibited from chasing after Mick again. He said I've wasted enough time trying to find him and the rest of our lives should be enjoying being together and working on our own family," Trudy confessed.

Andy, possibly feeling the tension said, "What's in the past is the past. Let's make a meal of the things I brought and whatever's in the kitchen before we jump in on sorting out the material and yarn."

Her sisters were willing to forget their differing opinions and joined in preparing a meal and putting a small roast into the oven for Bea later that evening. The sisters then started eagerly to disperse the material so each of them had projects to keep them busy.

The sisters got together every afternoon, Trudy rushing home to fix dinner for Preston while the other two, essentially widow's, ate dinner together while Andy always left before dark. Bea needed an early night to make up for the fact she wasn't able to get a nap in the afternoon with the sisters all working on their tasks.

Bea stopped worrying about the future and about finding Mick. She would plan her life around this child and its needs. She got a warm feeling every time she thought of holding this child in her arms, watching it smile and talk and walk. She remembered the twins as infants, of course, but she was a child herself at the time and their mother was still with them. This time it would be her taking care of the infant, with the twins' help, of course.

She would have the family she had been searching for and possibly it would be enough. Let memories of Mick and the life she thought they could have together fade, just as her memories of her mother had. She could barely remember what she looked like, what her voice sounded like reading to them, what she smelled like.

Now Bea had to be all those things for this little one she was going to give birth to. This child would never know loss or want for anything. Not even a father.

Bea felt warm and a soft exhale of breath on her cheek when she woke up enough to feel a heavy arm across her stomach. "Devlin, why are you in here?" she asked groggily.

"I got back and came in to let you know, but you were so deep in sleep I decided to lay down here with you until you woke up. I guess I fell asleep, too," he told his wife giving her cheek a kiss.

"What time is it? Is the sun even up, yet?" she asked not wanting to open her eyes to find out for herself.

"Hmmmm, no, we got hours yet," he said trying to lull her back to sleep while he stayed in her bed next to her.

Just then Devlin wide-eyed, asked, "What was that? Did the baby just kick my hand?"

"No, the baby kicked me then you felt it. Think about how hard it feels to me if you can feel it out here," she said not paying more attention to her husband's amazement than to the baby's attack.

Devlin settled back down. Letting his hand move over her stomach, trying to catch his child's kick or push when it occurred again. Then he was rewarded, another kick so he left his hand in that spot to see if he would again feel the little kick. A moment later there were two kicks and then a pressure against his palm as the baby stretched, trying to find more room in its tight little home.

"Oh, my God, Red, this baby is really going to town. You can feel all this, right?" he asked still trying to get his child to kick or push on his hand. She marveled at the fact that he was playing with this child that wasn't even born yet.

Bea had to move so she rolled over to her back,

which usually caused the baby to become more active, but this time she was hoping it would calm it down. It didn't.

"I have to get up or this baby will never settle. You don't want it to kick its way out do you?"

"That can't happen, can it? I mean, it's too early and it can't really get out, can it?" Devlin said becoming upset but seemingly trying not to cause Bea anymore distress.

"No, Devlin, I was teasing. The baby won't kick its way out. It will simply feel that way to me," she said getting up and heading for the water closet.

Devlin was right outside the door when she came out, worry plainly on his face. "Is everything all right?

"Everything is all right, Devlin, and I did meet with a doctor who suggested a midwife that he said was exceptionally good. So, I met with her, too. She told me what I already knew. That all is going as it should, but she questioned the date of conception. Since we both know it was one of two dates, I know I'm not wrong, but the baby seems to be big for its due date. I explained that you were rather large so she told me she'll plan on delivering a big baby. Thank you very much." She ended sarcastically as she crawled back into the bed and laid on her side again, the baby having settled down with her walking around.

Devlin laid back down behind her, spooning all the way to their feet. Bea was soon asleep, but he stayed awake worrying about his wife and that their baby was going to be bigger than average. Bea was tall but that didn't mean she would have any easier time delivering a large baby.

Devlin was worried. He knew many women died during childbirth and he didn't want to think Bea could be one of them.

The next week Devlin was mostly at home. He went out some afternoons but the twins weren't an everyday occurrence in the parlor anymore. Bea accompanied the twins to all their favorite stores and markets so became familiar with the neighborhood and what was available. She bought enough food for an army and proceeded to feed her husband three meals a day.

She returned to taking afternoon naps so that she was awake in the evening longer. She crocheted caps and a summer sweater for the baby while Devlin read files and studied wanted posters.

As the weeks passed, Bea finally couldn't prevent herself from asking, "Did you still plan to go to the poker contest to see if Mick would be playing? Do you have time?"

Devlin hoped his thoughts didn't show on his face as he laid down the sheets of drawings and replied, "I didn't forget, Red. I planned on going out tomorrow to be there when the attendees begin the sign in. I hope you know what you want, Bea. Once this guy gets into your life again it might be difficult to get him out."

Bea turned hurt eyes on her husband. "I thought you understood, Devlin. I will keep looking for Mick and give him every chance to take his rightful place with me. This isn't a fluke. I will always love him no matter what he decides to do with his life."

Devlin went back to reading the wanted posters, not seeing anything in front of his eyes, the pain that went deep into his soul making thinking, seeing difficult. He had to honor his promise, of course, but it would leave a bad taste in his mouth. His only hope would be that Mick would again reject Bea. She'd be hurt but Devlin would try to make it up to her.

He didn't feel he was being selfish or covetous. He loved Bea and could take good care of her and their children. He didn't have bad habits like gambling or drinking and would put his family ahead of everything including his job. When he felt it was detrimental to his family, he would quit and become a rancher again. He knew if Bea looked at it properly, she would accept him and perhaps he could make her love him half as well as she evidently loved Mick.

CHAPTER FIFTEEN

Devlin sat in the back of the casino that was to hold the many card players scheduled to participate in the next three days of gambling. He glared at each man as he entered the double doors at the other end of the long room, trying to see if any one of them would stand-out as the love of Bea's life. One was too old, the next too young. A few women came in on men's arms and fluttered their lashes and waved their gloved hands in the air when they saw someone they recognized. But Devlin wasn't interested in the women unless they were on the arm of one, Mick Elliot O'Malley.

Hours later, Devlin still watched the door. He was dressed the same as more than half the participants, suit with waistcoat, white starched shirt and black tie. Dress boots and black Homburg finished the outfit. Completely citified, no sign of the Texas marshal in sight, so he hadn't caused any concern for the gamblers be they honest or be they cheats.

A few of the women whose men were busy at the tables walked towards Devlin, but when his gaze didn't hold to theirs, they kept moving. Devlin was getting bored and frustrated. Mick wasn't going to show. Damn it, Devlin wanted an end to this, hopefully with Mick walking away from Bea. But Devlin was too honorable to go back and tell Bea that was what happened if it hadn't.

Then a tall slender man with auburn hair and brows walked in. Sure of his welcome, he smiled and nodded to almost every other man in the room. This one was well-known and well-liked. Several of the women gravitated to him and he greeted them with a kiss on cheeks, bestowing his largess near and wide.

Devlin felt this man's charisma from across the room and hated him. The man wore a brown and gold hound's tooth suit with plain gold waistcoat, a watch chain swinging from the pocket. Starched shirt and a dark brown tie wrapped twice around his neck. He also wore a brown Derby and polished shoes and the word dandy came immediately to Devlin's mind. He knew it was Mick and he realized how Bea would be unable to forget a man like this, a man who had probably played with her young heart and then moved on.

At least she hadn't given herself to him completely. She had saved herself for Devlin and see how well that turned out? Not his best moment, he thought, disgusted with himself.

Soon all the tables were filled, cigar smoke curling up from each like dancing snakes he had seen at a sideshow. The room was quiet, the tenseness not lessened as men made decisions that would rule the rest of their lives.

Watching from the sidelines, he studied the way Mick smiled and picked up each card, holding them close to his body like most of the others were doing. Mick's eyes, crinkled with amusement as if he knew a secret no one else did, scrutinized the reaction from each player as they reviewed their cards, and how they placed them in their hands.

He learned a lot about Mick watching him play and figured out Mick was the man who taught Bea everything she knew about cards and how to spot a cheater. Not that Mick was cheating, not here, not with this crowd, but he knew how to cheat, how to palm and switch and deal from the bottom.

Mick had been Bea's mentor and it made Devlin angry to think this man had tried to force Bea into a life of crime. No not force, but certainly encouraged. But what stopped him from taking Bea with him then? Why isn't she on his arm like some of these other women were with their men? Devlin had to think about that, which he did as he watched as men, one by one, dropped from the tables, throwing their cards in disgust or good grace depending on their temperament. There was a lot of potential for violence here and Devlin was glad his badge was tucked away in a pocket. He wasn't here to keep the peace.

O'Malley was one of the last men at the table, playing so that he remained a contender. Gathering his chips, he turned them in to be counted and recorded. No money left the room and no chips entered. Each man played with the same stake and the winner would take all. Security men, big and burly, stood around the perimeter of the room, bully clubs handy to make sure of that. Devlin got up and followed Mick at a discreet distance.

The hotels and saloons were full, some of the losers taking out their misery on the smaller gaming rooms in town. Mick settled at a table with friends and a bottle of whiskey. Irish of course, and soon had almost to a man drunk and nearly passed out. When that group couldn't hold a descent conversation, Mick ordered another bottle and moved to a table where the men had been sensible enough not to indulge so heavily.

Again, Mick continued to drink, glass for glass until there was no one left conscious at the second table. Devlin was beginning to worry about his being able to keep watch on Mick's antics when that man stood and said good evening to the men still able to hear him and went to his room at the hotel. Luckily the same hotel where Devlin had a room so both men climbed the stairs in unison and Devlin was able to note the room Mick entered with a key.

In the hotel's restaurant the next day, Devlin was enjoying a very good cup of coffee when Mick entered, winked at the girl waiting on customers and gave her his order, taking one of the many empty tables. It was too early for breakfast for most of the men and women there for the contest, but not for Mick. Devlin thought that interesting as he watched Mick plow through three eggs, slice of ham and a stack of flap-jacks with molasses syrup and what must have been a half-gallon of coffee.

Mick wiped his well-shaved face and flipped a coin at the girl as he left the dining room. Devlin stayed for a while longer, Mick wasn't going anywhere. He was due back to the tables in a few hours and there was time to confront the man. Besides, if Mick won, his answer to Devlin's question could be completely different.

Devlin found Mick quietly reading the newspaper in the hotel's lobby behind a large palm. Devlin continued walking as if he had a chair in mind and sat down with the paper he had already read and shook it out as if to read it. Hiding behind the paper, he was surprised when Mick addressed him.

"You're not signed in to play. Are you some sort of security?"

"Do I look like security?" Devlin countered with a question bending the paper enough to see his quarry.

"Your suit's very expensive, too expensive to be a Pinkerton, but maybe you're here to protect one man? Someone that expects an attack of some sort, maybe one who plays too close to the table?" Mick suggested.

"No, just came to see what all the fuss is about. I was in town for other reasons, meeting an old friend in a day or so," Devlin told the inquisitive man. Mick must have sensed Devlin's interest and was trying to define the danger level.

"Hmmm, as tight as these hotel rooms were to get, it's a wonder anyone besides players are staying here. I got mine reserved a year ago, when the contest was first announced," Mick said trying to catch Devlin in a lie.

"I must have gotten lucky then because I didn't reserve mine until a week or so ago." Let Mick make what he can from that, thought Devlin. He shook his paper again to straighten the sheets and to let Mick know he was done with the conversation.

Mick got up and left while Devlin had to stay and pretend to read the paper for the next half hour. He didn't want Mick to realize Devlin's only reason for being there was to watch him.

That evening, Devlin was in his position against the back wall when he spotted Mick come in, a blond on his arm that he kissed on the lips lightly as she left him to sit in the many chairs set out for spectators. Mick was wearing another snappy suit, in a rusty brown stripe and the same gold chained watch. He got his table assignment and then stopped before going to the table and turned, looked directly at Devlin, and nodded in acknowledgement of his presence.

Devlin smiled inwardly. This Mick is no slouch when it came to playing games. He knew Devlin was here for something or someone and Mick was trying to figure out what or who. Unable to find a link between himself and Devlin, he was coming up with nothing.

Devlin imagined Mick's face when Devlin finally tells him why he was there. Well, not the whole truth, of course, only that Bea sent him and she wanted to see Mick, to speak with him.

Then Devlin will drag him back to Lemmoxville in manacles if necessary, but Bea was going to have her talk with this man so that afterwards, she would be able to move on. Hopefully, choosing Devlin and their family. He didn't want to face the chance of seeing his child dragged between casinos and gambling contests through-out its life.

Mick played well, the smile always on his face whether he was gaining or losing, always pleasant with the dealer, always polite to the others at the table. Devlin still hated the man.

There were fewer players and fewer tables today in deference for the players no longer in the running. By the end of the evening another group of men were no longer playing, but Mick wasn't part of their number. He would be back the next day, the last day of gaming.

And like the evening before, Mick bought another bottle of Irish whiskey and found a table of willing participants in the saloon nearest the hotel. Devlin nursed his one glass of whiskey and watched, ignoring the women who tried to entice him upstairs with them. He gave them a crooked smile and a sight shake of his head. If he was ever going to be with a woman again, it would be Red. He didn't even glance at other women in the same way anymore.

Finally, Mick got up from the table of inebriated occupants and told the room good evening and went to the hotel, walking as straight as a sober nun. Devlin waited a few minutes before going to his room for some much-desired sleep and to think over how he was going to approach Mick about Bea.

The breakfast room was basically empty when Devlin sat down and ordered coffee. He watched the snow fall lightly through the window, hoping it wasn't going to come down any heavier. He wanted to leave town early the next morning, with or without Mick, preferably with. Devlin knew Bea wouldn't let it end until she had the opportunity to speak with the man.

This morning Mick came in wearing yet another suit and tie, the watch chain still in place, and ordered a large breakfast. Devlin shook his head wondering where the man put it all. He was far from fat and spent most of his time sitting at a gaming table or a dining table. Must be good family traits.

Again, Mick nodded at Devlin but continued to drink several more cups of coffee, while Devlin finished his second. The men left the dining room at the same time and Devlin, just to see the other man's reaction, asked, "That lady with you yesterday, is she someone special?"

Mick cocked his head and said, "She's not going to be the mother of my children or anything. You fancy her?"

"No, merely asking. Good luck in there today," Devlin said.

"There's no such thing as luck, just skill. And I've perfected my skill," he said in reply.

Devlin expected an answer such as that. Devlin visited a couple of stores and then went to the casino where the last session would begin. This time the spectators far outnumbered the players, more women there to commiserate with and console the losers.

Watching as the tables were whittled down to just six men at one table in the center of the room, even Devlin leaned forward to see better. The tension was high, more so among the spectators who evidently had gambled on who was going to come out the winner. Mick was still smiling and being polite to the other players while most of them were morose and sullen. As if they already knew the outcome and were simply going through the motions.

Like everyone else, Devlin watched each card as it was dealt, making sure the dealer hadn't been paid-off or the cards didn't show signs of being tampered with. Devlin, in particular, watched Mick knowing his ability to cheat without being caught, just as Bea and Trudy could.

Mick never wavered or hesitated. His bids were smart and he folded quickly when he didn't have a hand. Many men would bid merely to stay in the game, but then the odds would always win out and part of those hands would be losers no matter how long you stayed in.

Finally, it was down to Mick and a man from Kansas. Not a true Texan left and many of the spectators were disappointed but still interested in the play. Mick smiled a little wider at what might be the last hand dealt and then reined it in. He pushed in a large pile of chips the first round of bidding and then doubled it on the second. The other player was older and heavier, beads of sweat running down his temple to land in his mutton chop sideburns.

The older man folded leaving the pile of chips on the table to Mick who tipped his head and pulled them to his side. The next deal was a loss for both, no one able to open. The final deal was out and the older man, a smile on his face and a satisfied gleam in his eyes pushed everything in. Mick sat up and pushed his piles of chips in, as well. The older man slapped down three jacks and sat back with a smug expression on his face as a roar of approval went through the crowd. Mick smiled as if he were going to bow out, but instead flipped his cards over to show two kings and three sevens, full house and the winner.

The room irrupted into pandemonium while the other man swore and started accusing Mick of cheating. It would be the only way Mick could have won that hand, the older man said. Mick watched the other man intently.

All the players were supposed to leave their weapons off the gaming floor so Devlin stood up and placed himself close to the two gamblers. His badge predominately placed on his suit jacket, he said, "I've been watching everyone at this table as has the casino owner. There have been no illegal actions with this game. It was the luck of the draw." Then glancing at Mick finished, "And the skill of the players."

After the room finally cleared, Mick was still waiting with the casino owner and speaking of how they were going to transfer the funds so Mick wouldn't become a target. Neither man wanted anything to taint the contest or its future.

The casino owner turned to Devlin, saying, "I'm glad you were here, Marshal. I thought you were just an aficionado, but you defused a situation that could have gotten ugly. Some men shouldn't gamble if they can't lose gracefully."

"Well, I've had plenty of practice doing that and I have to admit it feels much better being a winner," Mick said, that grin appearing again. "Do you want to have a drink with me? Just one in the lobby? I don't usually drink after a win, it's not a way to celebrate. I used to go home and celebrate with my sister, but she's probably off and married with a passel of kids by now."

The two men were seated in a quiet area of the lobby, most of the contest's gamblers were either getting drunk to forget or getting drunk to remember. Mick held up his glass in a salute to Devlin. "Thanks for saving my ass, although I'm not sure he actually had a gun."

"He didn't," admitted Devlin. "His woman sitting right behind him did. I noticed it earlier but didn't want to cause a fuss simply because she was carrying a weapon. Of course, once her boyfriend became one of the last men at the table, I kept my eye on her."

"I thought you finally stopped focusing on me. You ever going to tell me really why I interest you? And I'm not worried that you like me a little too much. I'm not getting those kinds of looks from you," Mick told the much larger Devlin with a laugh.

"You're right, but I wanted to wait until after the contest. I didn't want to be blamed that I threw you off the game and made you lose." Devlin watched the other man's reaction, to see if anything seemed to come to mind. "Now it's all over I can tell you what an ass you are. That you have caused more pain than you could ever imagine. You are a selfish, single minded fool."

Mick thought it over for a moment nodding. "My sister, Bea, used to tell me much the same thing. I guess I just can't grow up."

Devlin jumped enough to slosh his drink saying loudly, "What did you just say? About your sister?"

Mick was surprised at the reaction his simple statement caused but then explained, "My sister,

Beatrice, used to tell me I was selfish because I wouldn't come back home. I just couldn't live with my father, but I shouldn't have abandoned my sisters to him even if I was too young to care for them properly."

"Your sister, Bea, what's she look like?" asked Devlin.

Mick closed his eyes as if picturing her. "She's a bean pole, tall with no shape at all. Bright red hair, all curls that she can never get under control. But the loveliest green eyes. She's going to be a beauty, well, probably is by now. I keep thinking of her as young and in short skirts, the twins, too, but they're all old enough to be married by now. If my father would ever approve of anyone enough to let them go. He likes the free cook and laundress although I warned Bea that as long as she acted as his housekeeper, Pa was never going to settle in one place and let the twins go to school."

"Mick, I have some information for you that may come as a surprise. Your father's been dead for several years and Bea and the twins have been following your trail from Kansas City to here. They now live in Lemmoxville less than ten hours away by train," Devlin said watching emotion travel across the younger man's face.

"Bea's been following me? But why?" Mick asked, not understanding what Devlin was saying.

"I don't know why. I thought you were an ex-lover, someone who had abandoned her but I was confused. You abandoned her, but you never loved her," Devlin said angrily.

"I loved, Bea. I love Bea still and the twins, but they were so young when I had to leave home. I felt one of us children should be out of jail when the old man got caught, to take care of the girls if it ever came to that," Mick said, his drink set aside as he thought about this new information regarding his sisters. "Are they all right? Are they safe? Do they need money or anything?"

"They are all well taken care of but they had an unusual life style the last few years while living on the road. Stopping long enough to build up a nest egg then travelling on when they heard you were seen somewhere."

"Do you think they'll want to see me now? I mean after so long?"

Devlin almost laughed then said honestly, "Bea is so insistent, I had to promise to bring you back. Even if I have to arrest you on some trumped-up charge. She's my wife and expecting our child in a couple of months so I don't have the option of denying her anything."

Mick stared at him in wonder asking, "You're my brother-in-law, then? And I'm to be an uncle. This is getting to be like a dream, everything too good to be true. And the twins? Are they living with you, also?"

"You need to come and see for yourself, but the twins are married, too. Andy married my deputy, Joshua Walker, and Trudy married a Pinkerton agent named, Preston George." Devlin watched the younger man take in all the information.

"That's a real joke on my father. He spent his whole life running and hiding from the law and his daughters bring three into the family. That's irony in the best form." Mick had a smile widening his lips as he sat back in the chair and enjoyed the paradox of having all those lawmen in the family.

"Preston's one of the best men if you need to follow the money. Fake paper and counterfeit bills are his specialty. Walker is a man I always want watching my back. Excellent tracker, good with a gun and an expert with the Bowie knife. Not that I'm telling you these things to threaten you or anything. Mostly to let you know your sisters are in excellent hands." Again, Devlin watched the emotion run across Mick's face.

"Who would have thought it years ago? They were just pretty little girls who enjoyed being read to and wanting to learn to dance," Mick told Devlin something he didn't know about his wife and sisters-in-law.

"So, will you accompany me to see your sisters or do I have to arrest you?" asked Devlin, relieved that Mick wasn't a competitor for him with Bea, or was he? Could Bea still decide to follow her brother city to city as she had their father? A misguided need to keep the family together, to care for the brother she feels needs her as her father had? Devlin hoped the baby would make Bea realize her duty was with Devlin and their child. They should be her priority now.

"Of course, I didn't know our father had died or I would have tracked the girls down. That's one of the reasons I travelled so far south, changed my name, to get out of the same arenas my father played in—and cheated in. He taught me to play cards the way he did. If you can't win, then add a card, deal from the bottom, mark cards, send your son around the table to tell you what the others have by using hand signals. I got sick of it and was afraid he'd get Bea into gambling, too, although girls weren't allowed in to gambling dens," Mick said, his face grimaced with remembered pain.

"But he did that anyway. Not cheating but she knows all the moves," Devlin said.

Mick asked hesitantly, "Did you meet her when you

arrested her or something?"

"No, she was working the casinos and gaming halls, trying to stay near to your field." When he noticed Mick close his eyes in denial, Devlin continued, "She never sold herself or your sisters. They worked as dealers only, never did anything to be ashamed of. They had their own sense of honor and all of us husbands are lucky to have married them."

Mick opened his eyes saying, "Thank you for telling me. I wouldn't want to hurt them by asking, but I couldn't live with myself if they had been reduced to doing what I know would be abhorrent to them."

Standing up, Devlin put his hand out to shake that of his brother-in-law. "I'm for my bed now. I plan on leaving on the seven o'clock in the morning to get back by evening. I don't mind telling you that I miss my wife."

"I'll be done with breakfast in time to get to the station. I miss your wife, too." And laughed at the expression crossing Devlin's face.

CHAPTER SIXTEEN

Walker and Andy arrived unannounced at Devlin's house and was a surprise to Bea who became very excited when Preston and Trudy arrived a few minutes later.

"This must mean Devlin found Mick. I'm so happy. I knew we'd finally find him. He couldn't stay in the shadows forever," said Bea almost hopping in happiness.

Andy worriedly watched her pregnant sister and urged, "Bea, keep calm. Devlin may simply want to tell us something important and only wanted to say it once. Don't put too much into this, he just asked for us to try to be here tonight. We may be together as support."

"What do you mean by that, Andy? Support? Why would I need support?" Bea searched the other faces and said, "Oh, you mean if he didn't find Mick or if he thinks Mick can't be found, that he's dead. But I would know if Mick were dead and I know he isn't. Don't worry. Mick isn't dead and Devlin has good news for me, for us. I just know it."

"May I make tea, Bea? It was a little nippy on the walk here," asked Andy.

"Of, course, I already have coffee made because that's all Devlin drinks and Mick was so attached to his cup of coffee, it was always next to him even while gambling," Bea confided and jumped when she heard boots scuffing on the front porch.

Devlin opened the front door smiling when he saw everyone made it in time then opened the door wider and announced, "The prodigal son comes home."

Bea was the first to Mick, hugging him and crying into his coat, then letting the twins at him while their husbands stood back letting their wives cry it out together with their brother.

Then Bea turned to Devlin and hugged him, letting him kiss her lips, several times before pulling themselves together enough to remember there were others in the room. No one seemed to notice except possibly Walker who only smiled and shook his head, realizing how far gone his boss and friend was with Bea.

After a little talk Andy, always the practical said, "Mick, you'll come home with us because we have a spare room all made up. Bea, we'll be back tomorrow morning for a late breakfast because by then Mick will need another one. It's his favorite meal and I remember how he always ate us out of hearth and home in the mornings."

"Still does," added Devlin with a smile and a hug to his wife who was sitting on the arm of his chair.

After everyone left for their homes and bed, Bea turned to her husband saying, "I don't know how to thank you. You went to so much trouble to bring my family back together and though I know Mick won't be able to stay here long, he will know where we are and we can visit each other whenever we want. That's all I can expect since we are all adults now."

As they were getting ready for bed, Devlin stood in the open doorway and asked, "Can I sleep with you tonight? Not for… not to do anything, but I missed you and I thought you might let me." He ended lamely he thought.

"Yes, you're as good as having a hot pan in the bed," she told him with a smile. "I missed you, too."

"You mean your cold feet missed me. I can accept that reason as long as I can stay once I get you warm."

He cuddled her to his chest, letting his hand lay possessively across the baby bulge.

"I'll see you in the morning, Devlin. And thank you. You've made me very happy." She let him glory in her appreciation while he felt the baby move under his palm as his wife slept.

As promised, Mick and Andy arrived for the second breakfast of the morning. Mick, sitting with a cup of coffee, smiled and talked with Bea as if it hadn't been years since they last saw one another.

"So why is it you've kept such a low profile? I haven't been able to catch up with you, only hear where you used to be," complained Bea.

"Well, I'm not interested in winning some farmer's entire inheritance or stripping a shop-keeper of his future like Pa was. I took my skill and only played others who knew what they were doing, other professionals. I can't say knowing how cheats work didn't save me more than once, but it's dangerous to call a man out even if you do know he's a double-dealer. If he's cheating others, that's a different story. I'd either let the guy know I knew what he was doing and if that didn't work, I'd make an announcement and show the table what was going on."

Bea placed her hand on Mick's arm. "Oh, Mick, that could be so dangerous for you. Some of those men hold a grudge."

Mick placed his hand over Bea's and admitted, "Sometimes I needed a fast horse but cheats learned not to play at my table. Eventually, I very rarely had to call anyone out and others wanted to play against me because they felt they had more of a chance at an honest table."

"Still, it worries me even now. I know you were rebelling against father and I still understand why you left in the first place, but why didn't you come back?" she asked the one question that bothered her the most while Andy and Devlin listened for the answer, too.

"I needed to get out from under Pa's reputation. It was getting around that his skills had nothing to do with good card playing, but mostly how to cheat without anyone catching him. I didn't want to be associated with that. I did mean to come back and get you, all of you," he said nodding to include Andy. "But I wasn't financially able to until recently. I didn't know father was dead until Devlin told me. After all, Pa had so many aliases who would know he died?"

"I tried to find you once the girls were able to travel with me, but by then I was following very old trails and you weren't always using your same name either," she admonished lightly.

"Sis, there's time when it's best not to have the men opposite you at the table know your real name." He showed them that grin that had won him so many hands, Devlin thought.

Bea said as bluntly as always, "Look, I know when the Irish is coming out in your blood so don't be trying to smile and grin your way out of this discussion. Are you going to disappear again or can we plan on seeing you for the holidays?"

"If there isn't a big game, I'll be here. I missed you, Bea, we were like two sides of a coin and I'm sorry I blew up at Pa and ended leaving you with him," he said seriously.

Andy spoke up saying, "Bea would never have left us. She was the only stable thing in the constant changes that was our life back then. She always made us remember you were out there, part of our family. We never blamed you for leaving, Mick. Bea explained Father was too impulsive and too wild and that he threw the dice too often and dealt from the bottom too many times."

The four of them spent the remainder of the day talking, remembering their mother although Andy said she had a vague memory of a beautiful redhead who spoke softly and smelled like cinnamon. Trudy arrived before noonday and Devlin felt an interloper and backed away, letting the siblings re-learn their relationships. By dinner, everyone had been in tears at one time or another, Trudy leading the way as usual.

The siblings finally were talked-out for the day and Andy took Mick home with her again and walked Trudy home with them. Bea made another breakfast and fed Devlin before saying, "I need to go to bed. I'll see you in the morning. Have a good night."

Devlin looked at his wife, hoping not to be turned away, and asked quietly, "Can I come in and sleep next to you?"

"Yes, Devlin, just like before." Bea let him know he wasn't to expect anything more.

"Let me re-stock the stove and I'll be right in," he said turning down the lamp in the kitchen.

Devlin spooned his wife, letting her cold feet lay against his own warm ones, his hand around her to touch her stomach. "Tell me about him," he said in her ear.

Bea didn't pretend to not know who he wanted to learn about. "Father loved us. He really did. Mother the most, of course, and her dying so young sent his world spinning. Here he was left with two half-grown children and the twins were little more than babies. I took over the care of the girls and the household, but soon Father thought we should move and then move again. I didn't realize why at the time, but later I knew it was because people were catching on that father was cheating," she told her husband now they were in the dark. He didn't want her to see the expression of disgust on his face that she had to live that way.

"I'm sorry you had so much to bear at such a young age. You missed out on your childhood and I can't explain how badly I feel about that," he said, kissing her cheek.

"Mick lost his childhood too, maybe more than I did because father thought Mick was the perfect foil to his personality. Actually, they were too much the same. Both were attractive without being threatening to other men. They had smiles that would melt a mother's heart and people, everyone, always liked them. No one saw what was coming. He justified himself by saying a man shouldn't bet more than he could afford to lose, yet he did every day. I can't tell you how many times we had to sneak out of our rooms because we couldn't pay the past due rent. I hated that part almost the worse. Those people, usually widows or older couples, needed our rent to live."

"You were a child yourself and not to blame for what your father did," he said trying to comfort his wife.

"I know, but when I knew what he was doing I should have found a way to make him quit, to live a life he could be proud of. I'm not sure he ever felt guilt or compassion for those he swindled. I mean he was good at what he did, but when the cards weren't going his way, he kind of steered them. I understand Mick's policy of only playing men who know the game, played because of the skill involved as well as a compulsion. Men who make gambling a career. They're used to the ups and downs and it's all just part of the game."

Devlin let her talk it out, opening new wounds and healing them with the next breath. The men in her younger life hadn't been evil, but driven by some inner demon to keep the cards on the table, jumping from one gaming hall to another. Unable to put down roots because they would run out of marks or money.

Bea stopped speaking, seemed to think about her childhood then continued, "I remember when Father would line us up at the dining room table and make coins disappear and re-appear, sometimes from our ears or have us pick cards and then no matter what, he would find our card again magically. Later he taught us those tricks, but as children, Mick and I would be amazed at how wonderful our father was. We thought, if anyone could walk on water, it would be him."

"You should remember that father, the one who raised you to become the wonderful woman you are today. You took over as the head of the family, you taught and cared for the twins, and you are growing my child. That's the woman you are and your father had a hand in forming you so don't think all ill of him. Everyone has their flaws and weaknesses." He kissed her cheek again finding it wet with tears. "Enough of these maudlin thoughts, darling, get some sleep and we'll see Mick again in the morning."

The next morning Mick told his sisters, to many tears, that he would be moving on to Austin. That another big game was being planned and the money was all heading there, that any other games in the state would be a waste of his time.

"I promise to come back. There's always dead time

between games," he reminded them.

"That's nice, you'll fill in with us during dead time," said Trudy petulantly.

"A man has to make a living and mine happens to be gambling which means I need to follow the money. Every top player will be there, they expect me. I've got a feeling they want to prove this last win was a fluke. They want to knock me down a peg or two. Just as I would if one of them had won." He laughed at his sisters' wide-eyed expression.

All three sisters and Devlin saw Mick off, again with promises to return and to send them a note every once in a while. Devlin walked his sisters-in-law home and then continued to his own home with his wife, knowing she was having a difficult time with having the brother she searched for so long leave her the second time.

CHAPTER SEVENTEEN

Devlin was home for the next week, so he spent most of his time with Bea, enjoying being a husband. One evening after dinner he heard Bea call out from the bathing room. The house had running water to the tub, but hot water had to be added after being heated on the stove, which they had heated earlier.

Stopping at the door before barging in, he asked, "Bea, do you need more hot water? Can I come in?"

"I can't get out, I'm too fat." Mourned a forlorn Bea from behind the door.

Devlin bit his lip so he didn't laugh at her answer then opening the door stepped in. There was his wife, in the tub of water that had probably cooled to the uncomfortable stage, her hair piled up onto her head with wet tendrils hanging down to her damp shoulders. The large orbs that were now her breasts bobbed on top of the opaque water hiding the rest of her.

"I've tried over and over, but I'm still unable to get out. I can't get any bigger or I won't even be able to bathe anymore." Tears of frustration formed as she tried to get her arms in position to push herself up and out. But simply couldn't do it.

"Here, let me help. I'm sure all women get to this point." He placed his arms under both of hers pulling her up as he stood.

Once Bea had her feet under her and was standing on the floor, Devlin grabbed the large towel and began to wrap her in it as he would a small child. Only she wasn't a child, she had all the womanly curves and then some. Devlin hadn't seen his wife naked since that first time they made love, which seemed like eons ago. He

180

patted the towel over her body, helping her get dry and then removed it to pull the voluminous sleeping gown over her head.

"There," he told her. "All better."

Bea didn't seem like she felt all better. "I'm getting so fat, I had to have Andy put on my shoes for me yesterday so we could go out. Nothing fits. I have two dresses that I tie on and I had to make those ties longer. And I still have months to go." Then angrily added, "Are you laughing, you big oaf? This is all your doing. If you weren't so big, this child would be a normal size." Then her tears came in profusion.

"I'm sorry. I'm sorry, I wasn't laughing at you I was smiling because I think you are so very beautiful, like a Madonna."

As Bea pushed him away, he had to hold her so that he could explain his words. "Really, I have never seen a woman more beautiful. You have my child inside of you. I'm humbled knowing I was responsible for this new life. Because I made love with you, there will be another child, a bit like you and a bit like me. I really can't describe how much I want to kiss your stomach, your breasts, the womanly parts of you I had too few moments of knowing." Then he kissed her stomach covered by the gown and rubbed his palms lightly over her swollen breasts and finished, "You are not laughable, but you make me exceedingly happy."

Seeming to feel a little better, she climbed into bed that evening. Devlin took his place right beside her as she lay on her side, the only position the baby allowed her to sleep in. Devlin didn't remind his wife of her size in any manner and soon they were both asleep.

Bea woke up to Devlin making noise in the kitchen

getting his breakfast as usual. "I made tea and have a couple of eggs ready for you, Red," he told her when she came out wearing one of the two dresses, she informed him still fit—somewhat.

"Walker was just here. He got a telegraph message and we'll need to be out of town again." Then he thought longer, "I can pass on this one. Stay here with you."

"Devlin, I will be fine. I still have almost eight more weeks. You can't stay home every time I get upset with my size. It's going to be a while before I can become slimmer. And one or the other of the twins is always with me during the day," she told him as she sipped her tea without the usual sugar.

Devlin added a spoonful of sugar to her cup and stirred it saying, "I'll go this time because it shouldn't take long. I'll be home before we know it."

Bea and Andy fell back into their normal schedule when Devlin and Walker left for an assignment. Andy missed her husband and questioned her older sister with her worries.

"I know Walker had been with other women before we were married and I understand that. His needs had to be met, even when he was on assignment and away from his home. But we haven't discussed the subject now, since we've been married." At Bea's down-turned brows Andy quickly said, "I don't think he's being unfaithful, or bedding anyone else or anything, but he's gone sometimes for weeks. Am I silly to worry? Do you worry that Devlin is, I mean, you know, bedding someone when he can't be with you at home?"

"I hadn't thought about it, Andy. Do you have reason to think they are visiting other women?" Bea asked, thinking about how long it had been since she and

Devlin had been intimate.

"Well, before we were married, Walker let me know he…" Here the always-blunt Andy hesitated then continued, "That he desired me and when he wasn't with me, he ached, hurt even. We never did anything about it, he never asked or I might have agreed. But he wanted to wait, just as Preston did, although Trudy said she would have bedded Preston if he had wanted her to."

"I guess I'm the only O'Malley who showed such bad judgment," Bea said ruefully. "I am glad you girls didn't follow my lead. Is Walker showing any signs of not, ah-h, desiring you when he gets back from these trips?"

"He seems to be, umm, happy to see me, you know. Very loving and sometimes wanting to stay in bed for an afternoon, but is that the same thing he's been doing while he was gone or has he been waiting for me?" Andy asked worriedly, and Andy wasn't one to ask such questions of anyone. Andy was usually one people asked questions of.

"I think Walker loves his wife very much and is very glad to see her again no matter what. I don't believe he's bedding anyone else. He's probably too busy missing you to even think about another woman."

"You think so? Then you think I'm worrying about nothing? Devlin hasn't indicated that Walker may have strayed while they were out?" Andy asked again.

"Why didn't you ask if Devlin has strayed?" asked Bea watching her sister closely.

"Oh, Bea, don't be ridiculous. Devlin is so in love with you he practically eats you up with his eyes when you enter the room. He isn't interested in any other woman when he has you to come home to." Andy shook her head at what she evidently thought was Bea's foolish idea.

As the girls finished their meal, Bea asked, "Would you accompany me to the midwife's this afternoon?"

"Sure. Then we can stop by for more yarn to crochet another sweater since I have time." Andy put on her winter bonnet and cape to walk with her older sister.

When they reached the midwife's house, Bea asked for a private consultation and as the door closed the midwife asked in her usual brogue, "Now, Dearie, what do ye be needin'? Nae pain or signs o' blood is there?"

Bea hastened to tell this kind lady, "Oh, no, I'm fine. I merely had a question, about my husband…well about being intimate with my husband. Is it still safe to do so, for the baby, I mean?"

"Ach, yes. Ye can keep beddin' yer man 'til labor begins if'n ye wants. Men don't stop their needs once they gets their wife wi' child, ye ken. Better he's home wi' ye than wi' some doxy o'er a saloon. Don't want him bringin' any o' them diseases home ta ye and the bairn," the midwife explained.

"So, it won't be harmful for the baby? That's my main concern," explained Bea one last time.

"Nae, Dearie, continue doin' what ye always been doin'. The bairn don't mind the rocking." The midwife cackled with laughter.

The sisters walked to the shop and then back home to be pleasantly surprised by Trudy joining them for the afternoon. The three made good time on their projects and Trudy and Andy left before dinner, leaving Bea to take an early night.

Bea woke up to the warm familiar arm over her stomach, a light kiss on her ear. "Sorry, Red, I didn't mean to wake you."

"How do you think I can sleep through a two-hundred-pound interloper in my bed?" she teased and snuggled down, then became aware of her husband's arousal, which he tried to keep from touching her.

"I don't weigh two hundred pounds, I'm only one-eighty-five at the heaviest," he said into her ear as he tried to get comfortable in the bed next to her.

"I went to the midwife today," Bea started the conversation she wasn't sure how to begin.

"Nothing's wrong is there? With you or the baby?" he asked worriedly, his hand covering the mound in front of her.

"No, no, we're both fine, but she did say, I mean, I asked her…" Then rushed on, "We can be together if you want." At Devlin's silence Bea went on, "She said it wouldn't hurt the baby."

Devlin expelled his held breath and asked, "She told you this or you asked her?"

"Does it matter?" Bea asked now embarrassed with her announcement.

"To me, it does. Do you want to be with me again? Like we were before?" he said quietly waiting for her answer. She knew instinctively it mattered a great deal to him.

"Andy was worried that Walker might be bedding other women when he leaves town. She said that a man has physical pain when he doesn't, you know, when he doesn't have access to a woman. I didn't know that. I didn't know that I may have caused you pain and I'm sorry," she finished in a whisper.

Devlin hadn't moved since she began this conversation, maybe she was wrong to have brought it up, or maybe she should have waited until morning when they could have seen each other. No, that would have been worse, Bea was sure of it. She could feel her face blazing with heat as it was.

"What did you have in mind?" he asked letting his hand move up to cup her breast, a place where she often found it when she woke in the mornings.

"I…I'm not sure. I was simply making sure it would be all right for you to do what you might want to do," she told him and he pressed his arousal against her consciously, this time making sure she felt him there.

"I want you to know I haven't been with another woman since months before we met and once I saw you, I didn't want another woman. I may not have treated you very well but I never meant for us to be a one-night bedding. I wasn't being honest with myself at the time. I didn't think it through, but I wanted you in my life for always. I missed telling you that part when I should have so you'll just have to believe me now."

Bea thought about what her husband said, rolling onto her back and facing him and then asked, "Where does that leave us now?"

"With me between a rock and a hard place. I love my wife, but you'll always have doubts about my motives. And I will always have doubts that if you hadn't become pregnant you would have left me without a backwards look." She knew he was being honest with her. Letting her know how unsure he was of her feelings for him.

"So, you don't want to make love with me?" she asked, knowing she was disappointed.

"I didn't say that, Red. I'm not a fool. I want you so badly I'm practically vibrating like a string overtightened on a fiddle. I can almost hear the hum. I just don't know if I can control myself. I don't want to scare you and I don't want to hurt the baby. I'm not sure I should plan on doing anything, yet."

"I don't think anything you do will scare me, Devlin, and the midwife said the baby would like the rocking," Bea admitted, giving Devlin the option to choose.

"I'd like the rocking, too," he admitted kissing his wife on the lips. "I can't say I haven't dreamt about this for so long." Deepening the kiss, he brought back the memories of their first illicit night together.

Bea responded with all her repressed desire, returning Devlin's passion as he gently molded her breasts and stroked his hand down her body. Bea pushed herself towards him, urging a firmer contact, a longer stroke, a more intimate touch.

He accommodated all her wants and needs, letting her know he was willing to do anything that felt right for her. Hearing her eager little pants, he brought her to a cataclysmic release. He followed with an explosion of his own, holding tightly to her still trembling body.

"My God, Red. You're going to be the death of me. I don't remember anything like that ever happening to me before." He kissed her as they both recovered.

"Maybe I should have spoken to the midwife about this sooner. I wasn't thinking like a wife, I guess," Bea confessed letting her husband pull her into his arms again. Spooning her into what had become their usual sleeping position.

"It doesn't matter, love. We haven't been a very typical couple so why would we have a typical romance? I'll tell you now though, I love you. You don't have to love me, but I do need you to let me love you and take care of you," Devlin finally admitted, pulling the blankets up over them both.

Snuggling down, Bea thought of what he said last. Did he only love her, feel the need to take care of her because she was carrying his child? He never mentioned love before and Bea didn't trust words said after the event. She kept her own counsel and went to sleep without responding to her husband's confession.

Bea woke up alone in the bed, hesitating to join Devlin in the kitchen where he would have stirred the stove into flames again to warm the house and get the coffee and tea made. Things he did every morning when he was there.

She liked getting up to a warm house so she couldn't complain and he always let her sleep in since he knew the baby kept her awake some nights.

"What did you want for breakfast, Red? There's still some of that ham on the porch, or bacon?" he offered not looking at his wife. Was he afraid of what he might see in her eyes?

"I'm not very hungry, but I'll fix you whatever you want. Go and sit down, I'll finish," she told him, taking the pan out of his hand. She peered up at him and he grinned back, there were no recriminations, no look of anger or blame. He leaned down and kissed her on her nose, watching her smile of pleasure as he went to do as she told him.

Bea felt more relaxed with her husband than she had since moving in with him weeks ago. Devlin stayed around the house and spoke with Preston when he dropped off Trudy to stay with Bea for the day. Andy and Walker were doing something together, taking advantage of the free day.

Both men told their wives goodbye and gave them a kiss, which she knew Trudy had noticed but didn't comment on. She seemed happy her older sister was settling into her new life as a wife and soon to be mother. Perhaps Bea would stay in Lemmoxville as Trudy and Andy hoped.

Bea was caught daydreaming several times by Trudy until that sister simply stopped talking and left Bea to her own thoughts. They had decided to start on a quilt, the wedding ring design, with pastel colors. It would be used on Trudy's bed, and then the plan was to sew one for Andy next. Bea hadn't asked for one so the twins refrained from making a big deal of it. She knew the twins had hoped things would change, and that they would be sewing three of the pretty quilts after all. Trudy could probably see that possibility now.

That evening as bedtime approached, Bea began to get agitated over the simplest things so Devlin pulled her onto his lap as she went by him once again.

"We've got to talk." She gazed into his eyes warily. "As much as I'd love to do what we did last night again, I don't want to appear greedy with your generosity. So, if it's all right with you, I think we should simply sleep tonight. Maybe I can hold you as usual."

"I don't know why it was making me edgy, but I was feeling as if we took too big a step at one time," Bea explained, allowing him to hold her to his chest so that she could hear his heart.

"I love you, Bea, don't forget that. I'm going to bathe so go on to bed and get a head start. You look tired. And there is the other reason I should let you rest. I kept you awake last night." He put Bea away from him so he could heat the water.

CHAPTER EIGHTEEN

As a couple of more weeks went by, Bea felt less able to do much around the house even with her sisters helping. They decided they needed more thread for the quilt and were now walking toward the shopping area.

Bea wasn't feeling very attractive with her swollen ankles and ungainly gait. "I get so winded so easily these days. I feel like I'm carrying a couple of watermelons all the time. And those are just my breasts!"

"Oh, Bea, don't make me laugh. It's too early in the morning and my belly will ache," Trudy said looking with commiseration at her much heavier older sister.

The realistic Andy added, "They're small watermelons, at least. All we have is a couple more blocks and then you can rest. Besides, the exercise is good for you."

The three continued to the small grassed area and Bea rested on the park bench. The last snow had been gone for a while and there were green buds on many of the bushes, the smell of spring in the air.

"There's several more weeks before Bea's confinement. We should get the men together when Walker and Devlin get back and have a picnic. Maybe out in the country, oh, and fishing. We can have the men catch our dinner," Trudy said excitedly.

Andy laughed. "I know Joshua can fish, probably Devlin too, but what makes you think Preston has ever fished?"

"I'll let you know, my husband is very talented and if he doesn't know how to fish, he'll find out how," Trudy said defensively.

"We're not questioning his manhood for goodness

sake. Only if he knew how to fish since he's lived in a city all his life and our husbands were raised in the country, on ranches," Andy explained.

"I don't know why men raised in the city should be thought of as less, I don't know, less manly. I'd bet Preston is more of a man than either of yours when it comes to doing, ah-h-h…." Here is where Trudy realized her mistake on taking on Andy in an argument. "Aa-h-h, things with his hands. Yes. Preston is really, really good when it comes to his hands." And she blushed furiously.

"Hmmm, I don't know if there is an experiment that we could perform to prove your theory. It would need to be based on personal experience and I'm sure we all think our husband is the winner. I think this is an argument that we will never have a concise answer to," admitted Andy to let her sister off the hook.

As the three returned closer to their homes, Bea stumbled and Andy caught her arm to keep her from falling.

"I'd say watch your step but I know you can't see your feet," teased Andy helping her sister regain her footing.

"I didn't trip, I got a twinge." She took a step leaving a wet trail and looked at Andy in shock. "I just lost my birthing-water. I need to get home, quickly. Help me."

Starting to run, Trudy said, "I'm going to get Preston, he should be working from home."

"I'll try to get her home, but I really don't think you should leave us," Andy told her twin.

Calling back, Trudy said, "Don't try to move her. Stay here and Preston will know what to do."

And he did.

Preston ran past Andy and swept Bea up into his

arms, meeting Trudy still trying to catch up with her husband. He called out orders. "One of you should probably get the midwife and one come with me to take Bea home. I don't know anything about these things, but I thought she wasn't due till mid-June," he said without getting winded even though Bea weighed quite a bit more than she once did.

"I'll get the midwife," Trudy said and broke away from the others heading in another direction.

"Devlin isn't in town, is he?" asked Preston as he carried Bea easily.

"No, I don't know when they'll be back. Walker didn't say." Andy was hurrying to keep pace with Preston's longer strides.

Once home, Andy took the key and opened the door, letting Preston and Bea through the door. "Take her to her room and I'll take things from there." Then to her older sister asked, "Is there any pain?"

"I've been trying to count, but I couldn't." Then stopped holding her breath while her sister held her hands.

"I'll keep track, Bea. Let's get you into your night gown and in bed and wait for the midwife to tell us what else to do." The practical Andy layered clean towels onto the sheet as she spoke.

The round little midwife came scurrying in, a large bag in her hand. "Now Dearie, what are ye' aboot getting' yer little sister so worried. Let's see now, ye best scoot down here ta me." She soon said, "Weel, Dearie, we will probably be seeing a wee one yet today. I ken ye was off on yer dates."

Bea shook her head knowing that she couldn't have been wrong on the dates but was that a problem? Did that mean it was too soon to be healthy for her baby? She tried to remember everything she knew about babies, which wasn't much. Finally fearing the answer, she asked, "If I'm right and the baby is only eight months, will it be healthy? Will it be all right?"

"Ach, don't ye be worrying aboot that, Dearie. Save yer worrying for when this wee one is goin' off in the world on its own. Not ta worry yet," the older woman said and both Andy and Bea tried not to focus on the early birth.

Hours progressed and the contractions came closer together and stronger, the midwife sat in a chair and knit a coat for her dog, although the cold weather was almost over.

"There's always next winter," she said optimistically.

Trudy went quickly into Preston's arms as she came out of the bedroom in tears saying, "Oh, Preston, she's in so much pain." He patted her back as he stared into the eyes of a tired and distraught Devlin who just came through the front door but heard it all.

"So, Bea's in labor? She's having the baby early?" he asked worriedly.

Trudy nodded. "The midwife thinks by midnight. It's too soon but she says babies come when babies come. I don't know what to do to help."

"What kind of midwife is she? Doesn't she even think that it's too early?" Devlin asked the room, rubbing one hand through his hair.

Andy came out of the bedroom saying, "I need to get more cold water to wipe Bea's forehead." Explaining her leaving the birthing room.

Walker went to her asking quietly, "Do you think

you should be in there with her?" But the question didn't get past the others' hearing.

Devlin asked, "Why shouldn't Andy be with Bea? Is she sick?"

Andy answered for Walker saying, "No, I'm perfectly healthy but I'm with child. I think Walker is simply being a husband." Then, reminding him of their wedding night repeated, "I don't scare easily."

"I'll go to her. If something bad happens, if the baby doesn't make it, I want to be there for her," he told the others, putting words to the fear they all had.

Devlin went into Bea's room, the shade pulled down to darken the room, now lit only by an oil lamp. He went directly to his wife in the bed, ignoring the midwife in the corner saying, "Love, let me stay with you. I won't get in the way, I promise."

Bea smiled saying, "Devlin, go out and drink coffee with the others or go down to the saloon. We'll send word when the baby is born."

Devlin was shaking his head the whole time she spoke, but before she could say anything more, she was caught by the next wave of pain, her eyes closing as she tried not to let out a peep.

"I'm not leaving, Bea. Here let me wipe your forehead. Can you drink anything? Tea?" he asked taking on the role of nursemaid. "Next time hold my hand. Is there anything that you think will help?" He wiped her perspiring skin with the cloth.

"Ye might git behind her when the wee one finally cooms. It helps sometimes ta push against something solid and ye looks ta be solid," the midwife said, startling Devlin.

"Just tell me when. Anything else?" he asked still

watching his wife, afraid she wasn't telling him everything.

"I think ye'll ken what she needs when she needs it. She's been frettin' with ye no here. She'll be better now, easier of ah mind. She can ha' ah wee bit of water or tea," the little round woman said.

Devlin saw Bea's eyes light up when she heard she could have tea so he turned to get it but Andy came in with more cold water to wash Bea's face. He sent that sister for sugared tea so he could remain next to his wife.

A few hours more and Bea was stoically enduring the pains which seemed to be almost constant.

"Is this because the baby's large? Is this why she's in so much pain?" Devlin finally asked the midwife, feeling guilty for being the reason Bea was in so much agony.

"Ach, nae. Big bairns gives the mother something ta push on. Nae, this is a first bairn and they always take a little more time. The bairns where it needs to be, now it can be anytime," she said, frightening and absolving Devlin in the same sentence.

"Bea, if you need to cry out, go ahead. It isn't going to scare me, do what you must," he urged his anguished wife as another concentrated pain began.

"I don't want my child to arrive into this world with me screaming. I'll get through this just fine. And so will my baby," Bea said as if saying it aloud would make it so. "But it's time I admitted to us both, I love you. I never meant to, but I love you."

Their gazes locked. "You know that is my dearest wish. Now let me help you birth our child."

Soon Devlin realized he could help most by sitting behind his wife and letting her push into him, her legs bent at the knees and her heels dug into the bed mattress.

"That's it, Dearie, the top o' the crown is showin'. A few more good pushes…. Wait for the contraction, Dearie, and then there, push with it. Yes, that was a nice one, now wait, and there it is, Dearie, another push and, yes, I have the head. Com'on and one more, and there we have it, a wee son ye have," the old crone announced happily.

Bea, lay back onto her husband as he leaned around her and kissed her cheek saying, "Thank you, Red, thank you. We have a son. You did it, love, and he sound's healthy."

Both parents were smiling, waiting as their son was wiped off and handed to Bea. She held him while they both inspected the loudly crying infant who had emerged from her body.

"Oh, Devlin, I can't believe we did this. He's beautiful, just perfect. I can't believe I have a son." Then bent forwards as if in pain.

"Jest the after-birth, Dearie. I explained it ta ye. I'll git rid o' it," said the older woman, stopping her other cleaning process to help the new mother.

Bea bent forward again, catching her breath in pain at the same time as the old crone cackled. "Dearie, I made a bit o' mistake here. It wasnae a large baby ye had in here, but two wee ones. Yer gonna get another child in jist a few minutes. Da, take that babe and place it ta the side there, but watch him so as he keeps breathin'. Then help ye wife ta birth another."

Devlin, once excited was immediately worried that Bea must go through another birth when she was so tired from this first one. Holding his wife through another contraction, he kept watching his son who was now quiet and seemed to be peering around, then gazed straight at him. Devlin held his breath realizing his son could see him or at least seemed to.

Bea was struggling, trying to catch her breath between the pains and Devlin realized she was about out of strength, that she was worn-out from so many hours of labor.

"Come on, Red. You can do it, love, I know you can. We have one handsome son already, let's see the other," he encouraged his wife.

Bea tried to smile, but it was lost in a grimace as another pain washed over her. Then it seemed like one long pain and there was another squall. Bea leaned back, starting to laugh as the second baby was wrapped and handed to her. This time when she unwrapped the baby, she discovered a daughter, a perfectly lovely girl.

Devlin laughed saying, "Well, there I go thinking only one way. I was thinking twins were always the same sex when I know differently. It never crossed my mind that we would get one of each right off the mark. Now the pressure is off us for the next time. We can have either."

"Oh, I have to wait a little before I can think of having another. Remember I already raised one set of twins," she said accepting her husband's kisses from behind her shoulder.

A light knock sounded on the door and Andy stuck her head in. "Is everything all right. We heard the baby and then it got quiet. Trudy is half-hysterical with fear so I thought I would come in to find out, but I see the baby is fine." She walked into the room to peek at the baby still in Bea's arms.

Then Devlin leaned over and scooped up his son and

said proudly, "Don't over-look the first born now, Andy. You can tell them we have one of each so you'll have to beat that."

"Oh, Bea, how wonderful. Twins. I don't know if I dare tell Walker, he's afraid of getting just one," said Andy. "Oh, yes, I forgot Bea doesn't probably know, but I'm expecting in about seven months. That is unless they're twins."

"Weel, I'ma warned now we ye gurls. I'll be watchin' for two at a time, I weel," said the midwife as she moved about the room.

Andy said, "Can I show him off, please? I'll bring him right back and then I'll take the girl. Oh, hurry up and name them so we'll all know." She carried the first born out to the rest of the waiting family.

Bea gazed at her husband. "We never did talk about names. The birth seemed so far away I thought we had weeks to decide."

"But now we can see them and that alone might help to name the little blighters." He laughed as his wife slapped at him with her free hand.

CHAPTER NINETEEN

Bending over his wife's prone body as she laid in the bed, Devlin tucked the baby close to a breast. "Here's David, Red, and he's hungry as usual. I'll walk Beth around until she's asleep. By then David should be ready to have his back patted."

"You're so good with them. Who could have guessed?" she teased her husband.

"Well, you met my parents. I had good examples," he said not meaning to malign her parents so added, "And so did you. You can't throw out years of good parenting simply because your father lost his way for a while. Like you told me, he always loved you and wanted to keep you near him. Not bad parenting motives at all."

"I know and I understand him more every day. I enjoyed meeting your parents when they visited. I know they were thrown off guard by the timing. They just learned we were married and then we hit them with twins. I wasn't sure how your mother would take everything. And the bassinet she brought is lovely, an heirloom for our children."

"Would you like to hire someone to help you? We could get a bigger place and a nurse or whatever they're called could live in and help with the twins."

"No, my mother handled two and so can I. It gets easier as they get on a schedule, really. All new parents get less sleep than they need, at least, for a while. I'll nap when they do," she assured him.

"I got the subtle hint Dad would retire if I wanted to take over the ranch. They would move to a smaller house built somewhere on the property. I told them I'd think about it," he said not really watching his wife.

"Is that what you want, Devlin?" she asked doubtfully.

"Don't know. Not sure. What about you? Could you see yourself as a rancher's wife? It gets a little lonely on a ranch."

"I want to be by my sisters so our twins will maybe grow-up with their children…but if you were a rancher, you'd be home most of the time, wouldn't you?" she said, touching the soft baby cheek in front of her.

"Yes, but I also would be if I accepted the sheriff's position here in town. They want to hire both Walker and myself when the present sheriff retires in a couple of months. Or I could work at the state level, but not going on assignments, only running things from Austin. I would take Walker with me and Preston could ask to be reassigned there as well."

"Sounds as if we need to have a family meeting. I'll try to set one up soon so we can have an idea what we will be doing." Bea handed off her son now he had finished suckling.

Sliding into bed after laying the sleeping babies back into the basinet, Devlin pulled his wife to him. "Have I told you lately that I love you?"

"Not since dinner or was it right before bedtime?"

"No matter, I'm not going to stop saying it," he said nuzzling his nose into her hair.

They settled down for the next few hours until hungry babies woke them again.

A word about the author...

Author Susan Payne loves the written word. All historical and centering on a couple finding love and a happy ever after together.
Please visit her at
http://www.authorsusanpayne.com
or
authorspayne@gmail.com

Thank you for purchasing
this publication of The Wild Rose Press, Inc.

For questions or more information
contact us at
info@thewildrosepress.com.

The Wild Rose Press, Inc.
www.thewildrosepress.com